Hank *felt* his blood stir
at *the* *look* in Ann's eyes.

It teased like a delicate spring breeze. He knew beyond a shadow of a doubt that Ann didn't mean it, probably wasn't even aware of its effect. Yet, acting on irresistible impulse, his arm circled her waist, and he pulled her down.

He watched the color rise in her cheeks, enjoyed the sudden, sharp catch of her breath.

Then he felt like a heel.

The woman had done nothing but welcome him into her home, and here he was, blatantly taunting her, deliberately trying to seduce her, when he knew perfectly well they were about as suited as a porcupine and an armadillo.

When would he learn that not every challenge had to be met, not every bet won?

When, he thought in disgust, would he learn to walk away before someone got hurt?

Dear Reader,

Welcome to the Silhouette **Special Edition**
experience! With your search for consistently
satisfying reading in mind, every month the authors
and editors of Silhouette **Special Edition** aim to offer
you a stimulating blend of deep emotions and high
romance.

The name Silhouette **Special Edition** and the
distinctive arch on the cover represent a
commitment—a commitment to bring you six
sensitive, substantial novels each month. In the
pages of a Silhouette **Special Edition**, compelling
true-to-life characters face riveting emotional
issues—and come out winners. Both celebrated
authors and newcomers to the series strive for depth
and dimension, vividness and warmth, in writing
these stories of living and loving in today's world.

The result, we hope, is romance you can believe in.
Deeply emotional, richly romantic, infinitely
rewarding—that's the Silhouette **Special Edition**
experience. Come share it with us—six times a
month!

From all the authors and editors of Silhouette
Special Edition,

Best wishes,

Leslie Kazanjian,
Senior Editor

SHERRYL WOODS
Tea and Destiny

Silhouette Special Edition

Published by Silhouette Books New York

America's Publisher of Contemporary Romance

SILHOUETTE BOOKS
300 East 42nd St., New York, N.Y. 10017

ISBN: 0-373-09595-3

First Silhouette Books printing May 1990

Printed in the U.S.A.

Books by Sherryl Woods

Silhouette Desire

Not at Eight, Darling #309
Yesterday's Love #329
Come Fly with Me #345
A Gift of Love #375
Can't Say No #431
Heartland #472
One Touch of Moondust #521

Silhouette Special Edition

Safe Harbor #425
Never Let Go #446
Edge of Forever #484
In Too Deep #522
Miss Liz's Passion #573
Tea and Destiny #595

SHERRYL WOODS

lives by the ocean, which, she says, provides daily inspiration for the romance in her soul. She further explains that her years as a television critic taught her about steamy plots and humor; her years as a travel editor took her to exotic locations; and her years as a crummy weekend tennis player taught her to stick with what she enjoyed most—writing. "What better way is there," Sherryl asks, "to combine all that experience than by creating romantic stories?"

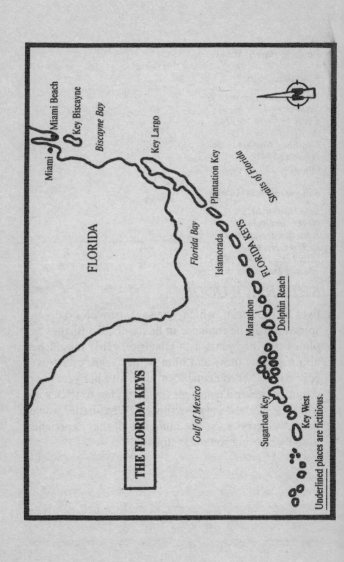

THE FLORIDA KEYS

Miami
Miami Beach
Key Biscayne
Biscayne Bay
FLORIDA
Key Largo
Plantation Key
Florida Bay
Straits of Florida
Islamorada
FLORIDA KEYS
Marathon
Dolphin Reach
Gulf of Mexico
Sugarloaf Key
Key West
Underlined places are fictitious.

Chapter One

It was already late Sunday afternoon when Hank pulled his pickup truck to the side of the narrow road, turned off the engine and stared. His gaze turned not to the spectacular red-tinted sunset in the west, but east, with a sort of fascinated horror, toward the worst-designed house he'd ever seen. As an engineer with a healthy respect for architecture, that house offended his sense of style, his sense of proportion, even his sense of color.

What had once been a small and probably quite pleasant waterfront cottage now lurched improbably across a tiny spit of land that poked into the Atlantic. Additions had been tacked on willy-nilly, adjusting to whatever natural obstacle had been in the way. One wing took a left turn away from the abrupt curve in the beach. Another detoured around a banyan tree.

Although it was all one story high, the rooftops were not level, as if the specifications for the additions had been dreamed up without paying the slightest attention to the original.

The color scheme... He shook his head in wonder. Was it possible that there had been only one can each of the salmon-pink, dusty blue and canary-yellow paint in the local paint store? The effect was jarring when it should have been soothing. The house reminded him of the owner.

Hank had met Ann Davies during the three days of festivities surrounding his best friend's wedding. Her effect on his system had been about as soothing as rubbing sandpaper across metal. Ann was a tall, rawboned woman with short black hair that he was convinced had been sheared off by a lawn mower. Her idea of makeup was apparently limited to a slash of lipstick across a generous mouth that was always in motion. The woman talked more than any other human being he'd ever met. She had opinions—strong opinions—on everything from football to mushrooms. She thought the former too brutal, the latter unappetizing. Hank loved them both.

So why, in the name of all that was holy, was he parked at the edge of her property? More to the point, what had possessed him to listen to his friends Todd and Liz when they'd suggested he come here? They had actually managed to persuade him—even before he'd finished the six-pack of his favorite beer they had settled in front of him—that he could survive in the same house with this irritating woman for the next few months while he supervised construction of a shopping center being built in nearby Marathon. They were crazy. He was crazier.

He was also desperate, he reminded himself with stark realism. It was early January in the Florida Keys, the worst possible time to be starting a construction job. Condos, houses and hotels were filled to overflowing with tourists. Those accommodations that were still available cost an arm and a leg. The company could have written off the expense, of course, but the few places still sitting empty weren't available long-term. They'd already been booked for scattered weeks of the season.

Even so, he'd looked at every one of them, hoping to find something that would do even short-term. Most consisted of nothing more than a tiny room and a shower. They were all too cramped by far for his big frame. He would have felt claustrophobic after a single night. He'd actually stepped into the shower stall in one and come close to being wedged in.

The remaining alternative, to commute from Miami, while not impossible, would have driven him nuts inside of a week. Traffic this time of the year required the patience of a saint. Hank recognized his limitations. He was no saint. Just the prospect of being locked bumper to bumper with a bunch of sight-seeing tourists made the muscles in the back of his neck knot.

Then Ann had offered, via Liz, to let him have a room in her spacious home at no charge. She'd even volunteered to throw in meals, if he'd pick up his share of the groceries. He couldn't imagine what sort of blackmail Liz had held over her to convince her to invite him.

"Why's she doing it?" he'd asked Liz suspiciously. "I didn't exactly charm the socks off her at the wedding."

He'd meant it quite literally. He'd never before known a woman who wore bright yellow socks and blue tennis shoes with a too-long green skirt and hot-pink T-shirt. Not even to the movies, much less to a wedding rehearsal. He shuddered at the memory. He should have known right then what this house would look like.

Liz had given him one of her serene smiles and said blithely, "Oh, you know how Ann is."

He didn't know. He didn't even want to. Yet the fact remained, here he was, a couple of suitcases in the back of the truck along with three bags of groceries he'd picked up at the supermarket. Actually it was two bags of food and one of beer and sodas. After a hot day on the job, nothing was better than lying peacefully in a hammock sipping an ice-cold can of beer. The soda was for breakfast. The carbonation and caffeine got his blood circulating. The sugar content of the jelly doughnuts he ate along with it gave him energy. He could have used both right now.

With one last fortifying breath, he turned on the ignition and drove into a driveway with ruts so deep they jarred his teeth. He pulled the truck around to the side of the house. He'd climbed out and was in the process of trying to adjust all three bags of groceries in his arms when he was slammed broadside by something that hit him about knee-high. The bags went flying. Hank grabbed for the beer the way a dying man reaches for a lifeline. He knew in his gut he was going to need that beer, probably before the night was out.

When he and the bag of beer were upright—the groceries were strewn across the lawn—he looked down and saw a child of about three staring solemnly up at him. She had a thumb poked in her mouth and a frayed blanket dangling from her other hand. He only barely resisted the urge to moan. He had forgotten about the kids. More likely, he'd conveniently blocked them right out of his mind.

Hank really hated kids. They made him nervous. They aroused all sorts of odd feelings of inadequacy. They were noisy, demanding and messy. They asked endless, unanswerable questions. They caused nothing but worry for their parents, aside from turning perfectly enjoyable life-styles upside down and inside out. Girls were even more of a mystery to him than boys. At least he'd been a boy once himself.

Still, he had to admit there was something appealing about this little girl. With her silver-blond hair curling in a wispy halo, she looked placid and innocent, as if she'd had absolutely nothing to do with virtually upending a man six times her size.

"Hi," he said cautiously. It had been a long time since Todd's son—his godson—had been this age, and he'd vowed to avoid Todd's new baby until she could speak intelligently. He'd figured that was another twelve to fourteen years away. He stared at the child in front of him. Beyond hello, what else did you say to a three-year-old, especially one who still had a thumb tucked in her mouth and showed no inclination to communicate?

"Where's your mommy?" he tried finally.

To his horror, tears welled up in the wide, blue eyes and the child took off at a run, dragging her thumb from her mouth long enough to let out a wail that would have wakened the dead.

Hank was just considering getting straight back into the pickup and bolting to the most expensive, tiniest condo he could find when a screen door slammed. The woman who'd loomed in his memory rounded a corner of the house at a run, her ankle-length purple skirt flapping, a butcher knife clutched threateningly in her raised hand. She skidded to a stop at the sight of him and slowly lowered the knife. Her furious expression calmed slightly.

There was nothing at all calm about his own reaction to the sight of her. His heart lurched with an astonishing thump. He dismissed the sensation at once as delayed panic. He'd rarely been confronted at the door by knife-wielding women. Surely that explained the surge of adrenaline that had his blood pumping fast and hard through his veins.

And yet... He took a good long look at her. Somehow all those uneven features he'd recalled had been rearranged into a face that was interesting, rather than plain, especially now with her color high. The tall, gaunt body, still dressed in an utterly absurd combination of colors and styles, seemed, for some peculiar reason, more appealing than he'd remembered. Her hair, still cropped short, suddenly seemed to suit her face with its feathery softness. It emphasized her eyes and those thick, sooty lashes. She looked... good. Damned good. Even with a knife in her hand.

He'd obviously lost his mind.

"Well, here you are," Ann said briskly as she put down the knife and began methodically to gather up the groceries. It gave her something to do to cover the nervous, fluttery feeling that had suddenly assailed her without warning. Nabbing a box of jelly doughnuts, she regarded them disapprovingly, then stuffed them in the bag along with assorted snack foods that she absolutely refused to have within a five-mile radius of the kids except on special occasions. She would deal with Hank Riley's dietary habits later, after she'd reconciled her memory of the obnoxious, arrogant man with the disconcertingly appealing sight of him.

"Sorry about Melissa," she apologized distractedly, fingering a head of lettuce. Lettuce was good. The choke hold this bearded giant of a man seemed to have over her senses was not. She swallowed hard. "I gather she's responsible for this."

"If she's about so high and partial to her thumb, she's the one," he acknowledged with a smile that made her stomach do an unexpected flip. "Did I frighten her or something? I asked where her mommy was and she let out a war whoop that would have straightened the hair on General Custer's head."

Ann struggled with the unfamiliar sensations that continued to rampage through her, decided her panic at Melissa's scream was to blame and reclaimed a bit of control.

"So that's it," she said, satisfied with the explanation for her nervousness and oblivious to Hank's confusion.

He was regarding her oddly. "That's what?"

She tried frantically to recall what he'd just said. Something about Melissa's mother and General Custer? She wasn't sure what Custer's connection was, but she understood precisely what had happened when Hank had mentioned the child's mother.

"I wondered what brought on all the tears. She came in crying about some man."

"Which explains the butcher knife."

She glanced down at the weapon she'd grabbed on her way out the door. It was lying at her feet. "Oh, sorry."

"Don't be. In this day and age, I don't suppose a woman can be too careful," he said, reaching down to pick it up. "Since you didn't use it on me, I gather you've decided I'm harmless."

Harmless? No less than a pit of vipers. How had she forgotten that he had this strange effect on her? All she'd recalled after the wedding had been his infuriating habit of contradicting every opinion she held.

"Maybe I'd better explain about Melissa's mother," she said, clinging to a neutral topic. "The woman abandoned her a year ago, just took off without a word to anyone. A neighbor found Melissa all alone the next day. They say children adjust pretty easily, but Melissa hasn't. She still wakes up in the middle of the night crying for her mother. Any reminder tends to set her off."

Professional training kept her tone matter-of-fact, but she still seethed inside when she thought about it. "It's beyond me how a mother could leave a child all alone like that. Anything could have happened to her. What if there'd been a fire? Good God, can you imagine?" she said, shuddering visibly. "Even waking up and being all alone would be enough to terrify a baby. When the social worker told me about it, I felt like going after the woman myself. No wonder Melissa's not adjusting."

Hank muttered what sounded like an indignant curse under his breath, then said, "I'm sorry. I had no idea. I guess I was just thinking of you as her mother."

"We don't do a lot of swearing around here," she warned automatically. "The kids, well, some of them anyway, are at that impressionable age. As for Melissa, she calls me Ann. Some of the kids refer to me as Mother. It all depends on what they're comfortable with. Since you're going to be here awhile, I'll give you a rundown on each of them, so you'll understand how they ended up here. The older ones are pretty open about things, but the little ones are still a little sensitive." She fingered a package of cupcakes, regarded them distastefully and sighed. "Then there's Jason. He rarely talks at all."

Hank didn't seem to notice the fact that she couldn't shut up. In fact, he looked decidedly uneasy. "How many are there?" he asked, as if he were inquiring about enemy troops just beyond a strategic hill.

"Five. Six. It depends on whether Tracy stays with friends after her classes at the junior college in Key West. Tonight they're all here. Occasionally one of the kids who used to live here comes back for a visit."

Hank, a man who struck her as big enough and tough enough to fear nothing, seemed to take a panicky step closer to his truck. He looked as though he wanted to escape. She could relate to the feeling. She'd felt that way since the instant she'd spotted him standing in the yard in faded jeans, a body-hugging T-shirt and sneakers. He hadn't seemed nearly as devastating in the suits he'd worn the weekend of the wedding.

"I probably won't see all that much of them," he said, an edge of desperation in his voice. "I'll be working pretty long hours."

She waved aside the objection. "Nonetheless, it'll be better if you know. Come on in now and I'll show you around."

She led him in through the kitchen, simply because it was closest. It was also a mess, as it always was by Sunday night after a weekend of having everyone at home. She saw Hank's eyes widen at the sight of dishes stacked all over the counter and tried to view the clutter from the perspective of a bachelor who probably paid a maid to do his housework.

Toys were scattered all over the floor and her papers were strewn across the round oak table that could seat ten easily and usually was surrounded by that many or more, all trying to talk at once. It was chaotic, but she loved the happy confusion. She could understand, though, how it might seem daunting and disorganized to an outsider. She shrugged. He'd just have to get used to it.

"We have cleanup in another hour," she said, stepping over a toy tank and rolling a tricycle out of their path as she plopped the groceries on top of the stove. "It's hard to imagine now, but by the time we sit down to dinner, this room will be spotless. Look quick, though, because it'll only be that way about twenty minutes."

Hank was still standing uncertainly in the doorway. "Are you sure I'm not putting you out? I know you told Liz it would be okay, but . . ." He waved a hand around the room. "You seem to have enough on your hands."

"Can you do your own laundry?"

"Yes, but . . ."

"Make your own bed?"

"Of course, but . . ."

"Are you any good at making coffee?"

"Yes, but . . ."

"Then it's no problem."

Almost as soon as the words were out of her mouth, Ann regretted them. If he wanted to run for his life, she should have let him. She should have encouraged him.

When Liz had first approached her about helping Hank out, she'd been adamantly against it. The man was the epitome of everything she disliked in the male of the species. He was handsome in some indefinable way that made him all the more dangerous. He had the powerful shoulders and chest of a lumberjack. He managed to have a light tan on slightly freckled skin that by all rights should only turn beet red in the sun. His hair and beard were a golden shade just shy of red. He had laughing blue eyes that could undress a woman in ten seconds flat, usually before the introductions were completed. He was bold and brash and irritating. His treatment of women had all the finesse of the caveman's, yet they flocked to do his bidding. With a reaction that was part astonishment, part dismay, she'd observed his effect on them at the wedding.

To top it off, his opinions on most subjects were diametrically opposed to her own. At the rehearsal dinner they'd been barely civil to each other. Their introduction had quickly escalated from hello into an argument about something so inane she couldn't even recall it now. It might have had something to do with the hors d'oeuvres. Liz had witnessed the clashes with interest, which made her plea to Ann for help all the more unbelievable. Ann realized later it should have made her suspicious at once.

"Think of him as a project," Liz had challenged. "You'll have weeks to work on him."

"I have six kids staying with me, plus a full-time career. I don't need a project. I need a maid."

"You need a man."

"Oh, no, you don't," Ann said, just catching on to the direction of her friend's devious thoughts. "Just because you're crazy in love and radiantly happy doesn't mean that everyone aspires to the same state of marital bliss. I do not need a man. I especially do not need a man who thinks that watching wrestling is cultural."

Liz had laughed. "Hank does not watch wrestling."

"Okay, maybe it was tractor pulls."

"You're just a coward."

"Hardly. I just don't have time to waste trying to rehabilitate a thirty-seven-year-old man. It's too late."

"You're a psychologist. You know perfectly well it's never too late to reform someone."

"If they want to be reformed. What gives you the idea that Hank Riley has any desire to change?"

"Think of it as an experiment. You could probably get a great research paper out of it."

"You're stretching, Liz."

"I'm desperate," Liz had admitted finally. "I already told him you'd do it."

"Why on earth would you do that?"

"It was a calculated risk. When have you ever turned down a stray?"

"Hank Riley has a home to go to. From everything you've told me and my own observations, he has more women to look after him than Hugh Hefner did before his wedding. He does not need me."

Liz merely smiled. Ann found the reaction irritating. And, unfortunately, challenging.

"Maybe you're the one I should be trying to reform," Ann had finally said with a sigh of resignation. "Send him on. I suppose it won't kill Jason and Paul to share a room for a couple of weeks. I'll put Hank in Jason's room. It'll probably give him nightmares with all those awful sci-fi posters on the walls." That thought had cheered her considerably.

Liz, however, had looked very guilty. It had left her virtually tongue-tied for just long enough to panic Ann.

"Okay, Liz. What is it you're not telling me?"

"Now don't be upset," Liz pleaded. "You can still back out if you really want to."

She buried her face in her hands. "Oh, Lord. It must be even worse than I thought." She peeked. "Okay. Out with the rest of it."

"It's just that it's more like a couple of months, actually. Maybe three or four."

Ann had protested loudly at that, but she'd known she was beaten. There were moments when she'd even convinced herself it would be just fine. It would be good for the boys to have a male role model around. Not that Hank was the one she would have chosen, of course, but a little of that macho nature of his might be okay for them for a short time. He could take them fishing, play baseball. She could do those things perfectly well herself, but she knew in her heart it probably wasn't the same. Whole textbooks had been written on a boy's need for male bonding.

Now that Hank was actually here in the kitchen, though, she wondered. He seemed a little overwhelming somehow. At the wedding, he had infuriated her with such frequency that she'd barely noticed that he had an interesting effect on her pulse. She'd assumed that it had been part of her constant exasperation with him, but he'd done nothing in the past five minutes to flat out annoy her and her heart was reacting peculiarly just the same. Maybe it was the sight of all those empty calories—doughnuts, potato chips, corn curls.

"These have to go," she said, taking a handful of packages and reaching for the garbage can.

Hank snatched them away from her, an expression of horror on his face. Indignation radiated from every considerable inch of him. "Are you out of your everlovin' mind, woman? Liz said you wanted groceries. I brought groceries."

"You brought junk. The kids will all be hyperactive if they eat that."

"So tell 'em not to touch the stuff. I'll sacrifice. I'll eat every last chip myself."

"You can't tell children not to eat foods like that, then put them right smack in front of them."

"I'll hide every bit of it in my room."

"See," she said, waving a finger under his nose. "That is exactly what I mean. You're addicted to that junk. That's what it does to you."

His blue eyes took on a challenging glint. "I enjoy it. I am not addicted to it. There's a difference."

"Smokers enjoy their cigarettes, too. That doesn't mean they're any less addicted."

He took one step toward her, which put them toe-to-toe. Close enough for her to smell the minty freshness of his breath and the clean, masculine scent of his soap. Near enough to kiss. Oh, dear heaven.

"The food stays," he said softly.

That gleam in his eyes turned dangerous. It might have been a warning about those damn corn curls, but she had a feeling it was something else entirely. She wasn't particularly crazy about the alternative. She took a step backward, then lifted her chin to counter any impression of retreat.

"Keep them out of sight of the children."

He grinned. "Yes, ma'am."

The response was polite enough, but the bold and brash tone made her want to slap him. Hard. She was shocked by the intensity of her desire to strike that smug, unrepentant expression off his face. She was a trained psychologist, a woman who believed in rational thought and the importance of calm communication. She did not believe in spankings for childish misbehavior, much less in beating up on people just because they infuriated her.

"Anything else?" he inquired.

She bit back a whole string of charges about his attitude. He was Liz's friend. Well, more precisely he was Todd's friend, but she would tolerate him just the same. He was only a temporary boarder, after all. With any luck he'd chafe at the restrictions of living with them and be gone by the following weekend.

"Dinner's at seven. We all help. House rule."

"No problem."

"There are others. Rules are important, especially for kids who aren't used to having anyone around who cares enough to enforce them. I'll explain them as the occasions arise." She tried her best to make it sound as though the household adhered to strict military discipline.

"Whatever you say."

She hadn't expected him to be quite so agreeable. For some reason, it increased her irritation. She nodded curtly. "Then I'll show you to your room."

Before they could even gather up his suitcases, though, there was another of those bloodcurdling yelps from the far side of the house. Ann dropped the bag she was holding and took off at a run.

"Does everyone in this house do that?" Hank said, sprinting after her.

"Only when disaster strikes." She hoped that sounded sufficiently ominous to terrify him.

"Does it strike often?" he inquired with what sounded more like curiosity than panic.

"If it makes you nervous—" she began.

"It does not make me nervous. I'm just worried it might be bad for their lungs."

"Their lungs are very healthy, except maybe for Paul's. He's had a few too many colds this winter." She paused in midstep. "I wonder why that is?"

Hank looked confused. "Why what is?"

"Why Paul was the only one to get so many colds?"

"Is this something you really need to figure out now? Shouldn't we find out why someone screamed?"

"Right." She turned a corner into the west wing of the house. "My guess is that the tub is overflowing. Sometimes the faucet leaks and the drain stops up. When both things happen together, well, you can imagine."

As if to prove her point, her sneaker-clad feet hit a wet patch of floor and shot out from under her. Hank grabbed her from behind and held her upright. She enjoyed the sensation of his hands on her waist far too much. She was almost disappointed when he released her. It was not a good sign.

"Stay here," he ordered in the tone of a man used to taking charge. That tone snapped her back to reality. She immediately bristled when he added, "I'll take care of it."

As if she needed him to, she thought with well-honed defensiveness. "I can handle it," she said, stepping past him and immediately skidding again.

"Stay put before you break your neck."

Leaving her sputtering indignantly, he waded off through water that was already soaking the hallway rugs. She glared after him. She could either make an utter ass of herself by arguing or she could do the pragmatic thing and help. Life had taught her the importance of being pragmatic.

She grabbed up the rugs and took them outside, then ran back for a mop. She was trying to stem the flow of water when Hank emerged from the bathroom with Melissa and Tommy wrapped in towels and tucked awkwardly under his arms like a couple of sacks of grain. He looked decidedly nervous. He handed them over as if he couldn't get rid of them fast enough.

"I'm going to get a couple of tools out of the truck. You might want to find some dry clothes for these two."

"Where's Tracy?"

"I left her figuratively holding her finger in the dike. Other than her hysterical scream, she keeps a pretty cool head in a crisis. This could have been a lot worse."

"She's used to it. The tub overflows about twice a week."

Melissa and Tommy, who'd seemed tongue-tied until now, began chattering enthusiastically about splashing through the water. Unfortunately it had become their favorite form of recreation. Ann had a suspicion they were secretly delighted every time the blasted tub overflowed. Hank listened to their excited stories and shook his head.

"Hasn't it occurred to you to call a plumber?"

It had. She'd dismissed it as too costly. She was not about to admit that to him. "The thought has crossed my mind, but I thought I could handle it myself."

"If you handle it any more effectively, you'll have to replace all these wooden floors."

His sarcasm set her teeth on edge. "Mr. Riley, may I remind you that you are a guest in this house. I do not need you to come in here and start telling me how to run my life or fix my house."

"Any more than I need you telling me what to eat," he retorted, matching her hands-on-hips stance. She had to admit he was better at it than she was. He was also grinning, which was not one bit like what she felt like doing.

"Okay," she snapped back. "Eat what you darn well please."

"I will."

"And I'll fix my own darn tub."

His smile widened. Then to her amazement, he backed down so fast it left her head reeling. "As you like," he said pleasantly. He waded off through the water, leaving her gaping after him. She was left with a throatful of angry words and no target at which to spew them.

"Where are you going?" she shouted at his retreating back.

He turned around and shot her a lazy, carefree grin. "I thought I'd have a beer. What about you? Want one? I could pour it while you're working on the tub."

"Go to..."

He halted her in midsentence by gesturing toward the suddenly silent, wide-eyed children standing beside her. "Tsk, tsk, Annie. No swearing in front of the children. Isn't that what you told me?"

As he disappeared from view, she wondered exactly how traumatic it would be for the kids to watch her take a shotgun to their houseguest.

Chapter Two

Ann was horrified. The serene, in-control woman she had always thought herself to be did not yell at the top of her lungs in anger. She did not consider using a shotgun to settle an argument. For that matter, until this afternoon, she'd never lifted a butcher knife except to slice a turkey. What was Hank Riley doing to her?

Bewildered and still fuming, she felt a tug on her skirt and looked down into Tommy's dark, troubled eyes. She was promptly overcome by guilt on top of everything else. She knew how much violence Tommy had endured in his first three years in war-torn El Salvador. For the two years that he'd been with her, she'd tried very hard to protect him from irrational outbursts. Even with seven very different people in the house, she'd been able to maintain an atmosphere of relative calm. Her own temper was blessedly even.

Until today, she reminded herself. In less than an hour Hank Riley had shaken her normal aplomb to its very foundations. That made her very nervous. She knew perfectly well that any man who aroused that much fury could probably arouse an equal amount of passion.

When hell freezes over, she declared, just as Tommy tugged again and asked in his softly accented voice, "Is he the plumber?"

"No, he is not the damn plumber," she snapped irritably, then immediately felt contrite. She hugged the dark-haired boy who was watching her with eyes that were far too serious.

"Sorry, baby," she said to Tommy as Melissa happily singsonged, "Bad word. Bad word."

Ann considered uttering a whole string of them. Instead she patted the child on her blond head and admitted, "That's right. That is a bad word and I don't ever want to hear any of you using it. You two go on to your rooms and put on some dry clothes."

"Want to swim," Melissa protested, her face screwing up in readiness for a good cry.

"You will not swim for an entire week if you two are not in your rooms by the time I count to three," Ann said very quietly.

They recognized the no-nonsense tone. Melissa's pout faded at once. Tommy was already scampering down the hall, favoring the leg that had been shattered two years ago by guerrilla gunfire. Ann sighed as she watched them go. Another crisis averted. Barely.

"Ann." Tracy's plaintive voice reached her. "I can't stay like this much longer."

"Oh, good heavens!" She ran into the bathroom and found Tracy exactly as Hank had left her, with her finger stuck at an awkward angle in the leaking faucet.

"Didn't the man even have sense enough to cut off the water?" she grumbled, turning back toward the door. The man in question was standing in her way, arms folded across a chest that could have blocked for offense on the Miami Dolphins.

"The water's off," he said, apparently unperturbed by her scowl or her denigrating comment.

"Oh."

She glanced at Tracy. "You can let go now."

Tracy shook her head. "That's just it. I can't. My finger's stuck."

With an impatient, you-should-have-known glance in Ann's direction, Hank stepped through the remaining puddles and sat down next to Tracy on the edge of the tub. Using a bar of soap, he worked Tracy's finger loose from the faucet. Ann was astounded by his teasing reassurances. She was even more startled by his gentleness. When Tracy's swollen finger was freed at last, he wiped it with a damp cloth, inspected it for cuts, then thanked her.

"You did a great job. Without your quick thinking, this could have been a lot worse."

Tracy beamed. Ann felt an odd fluttering in her chest. She hadn't seen a smile like that on the girl's face in all the years she'd lived there. Usually Tracy was far too quiet and unresponsive, except when she was taking care of the littlest kids. Her inability to get through to Tracy worried her. The ease with which Hank had astonished her.

"Honey, are you okay?" Ann asked, kneeling down in front of her, oblivious to the fact that her skirt was dragging in the puddles.

Tracy turned the radiant smile on her. "Sure." She held out her hand. "Not even a scratch."

"Great. Would you go check on Melissa and Tommy for me? After that try to get Paul and David to start cleaning up the kitchen. It's almost time to start dinner. I'll be there in a minute."

"Sure, Ann." She looked hesitantly at Hank. "Are you sticking around?"

"Yep." He shot a challenging look at Ann. "At least through dinner."

When Tracy had gone, Ann got to her feet and quickly began mopping up the floor, her soaked skirt slapping soggily against her legs. She couldn't quite bring herself to look at Hank, who was still perched on the edge of the tub fiddling with the faucet.

"You were very good with her," she finally conceded. "Thanks."

He didn't look up. "She seems like a good kid," he murmured, then began working a snakelike device down into the drain.

"Beware of calling an eighteen-year-old a kid. That's an offense considered on a par with listening to phone calls or denying use of the car."

"Umm." He gave a tug on his probe, which emerged with a small plastic dinosaur. Ann recognized it as one of Tommy's collection from the zoo.

Hank shook his head, tossed the toy aside and went back to poking around. "Sounds like you know her pretty well."

"I know teenagers pretty well. I'm not so sure about Tracy."

"She's not yours?"

Ann shook her head, instantly feeling a familiar defensiveness steal over her. "None of them are mine, not in the biological sense. I thought Liz explained."

"Only in the vaguest terms. She said you had several children you'd taken in. I assumed that some of the others might be yours."

"No. I've never been married."

That brought his head up, eyes twinkling. He gave her a grin that was only one quirk of the lips short of being a leer. "From what I hear that's not a requirement."

"It is for me," she said stiffly.

He studied her intently. "I see."

"I doubt it."

"Is your sexual hang-up something we should explore?" he inquired in a tone that teased and infuriated.

"I do not have a sexual hang-up," she said with slow emphasis, her temper reaching an immediate boil again. "And don't try playing psychologist with me, Mr. Riley. I'm the expert, remember?"

The grin faded. "How could I forget."

She listened for an edge of sarcasm, but couldn't detect one. An irrational part of her wished that grin were back, though.

"Tell me about Tracy," he said.

The ease with which he switched from provocative teasing to less dangerous turf irritated her almost as much as the teasing itself. Okay, she'd be the first to admit that she'd gotten out of the habit of taking sexual banter in stride, but she wasn't exactly the prude he'd implied. She was inclined to tell him just that, but reminded herself that she owed him no explanations. Instead she took the safe out he'd offered and said succinctly, "Tracy had some problems at home."

That was like saying World War II had been a small military skirmish. At the memory of the psychological and physical pain Tracy had suffered at the hands of an abusive father and a lousy system, Ann felt a familiar weariness steal through her. Apparently Hank caught her shift in mood.

"Bad, huh?" he said with quick understanding and a level of compassion that surprised her.

She stared into eyes that invited confidences and offered strength. "Lousy," she admitted. "Though I confess at times I forget just how bad it was for her. She tends to keep it all bottled up under a tough facade. Nothing I've done seems to get through to her."

"Was she a runaway?"

"I never thought I'd say this, but I wish she had been. Maybe there would have been fewer scars."

"You know that's not true," he said, glancing up. Blue eyes rebuked her. "All you have to do is ride around a few areas in Miami to see what happens to kids on their own too young."

She sighed. "I know you're right. Loss of innocence is pretty crummy at any age, but I doubt if Tracy ever had any innocence. She had a father who...well,

I'm sure you get the idea. He wasn't fit to raise pigs. He cast a long shadow. She's been away from there for nearly five years now and she's still not very trusting around men. In fact, she's pretty wary of all adults, probably because she thinks we all failed her."

"Can you blame her?"

"Not for a minute. That doesn't make it any easier when she's treating me like I'm the enemy, when all I want to do is help. Occasionally it wears me down."

"She's stuck around, hasn't she? You must be doing something right."

"Maybe," she said, though she was pleased by his observation. If he could see it, maybe she had been slowly winning Tracy's trust, after all. Though the girl often stormed out with a chip on her shoulder, she always returned and she always abided by the rules. Of all of them, in fact, Tracy was the one who seemed most in need of the reassurance that someone cared what she did—or didn't do. How odd that it had taken this virtual stranger with the penetrating gaze and quicksilver mood changes to make her realize that.

Suddenly the bathroom seemed too confining. Or perhaps it was simply that Hank's body seemed too masculine, too overwhelming, in the intimate space. It reminded Ann in an unrelenting way that she was a woman, something she all too often allowed herself to forget during jam-packed days of counseling and surrogate mothering.

"Why don't you go on and get settled?" she suggested, feeling a sudden need to reclaim some of her own space. "I'll finish cleaning up in here."

"I want to check out these pipes first."

"Don't bother. I'll call the plumber in the morning."

"Why should you do that? I'm here now."

"Then I'll pay you."

"You will not."

Ann's temper flared irrationally at his stubborn insistence. "Dammit, I will not have you coming in here challenging my independence!"

To her chagrin, Hank laughed. The sound echoed off the tile walls. "Is that what I'm doing? It must be on shaky ground."

Fury teased at her insides before she, too, finally chuckled. The tension in her shoulders eased. "Okay. That's a slight overstatement. But you do need to understand that I'm used to being on my own. It's important to me."

"I'll try not to trample on your liberated sensibilities, but you need to understand that for as long as I'm here I want to do my share. The kids have chores. Why shouldn't I?"

She lifted her chin to a defiant tilt. "The kids are staying," she pointed out. "You're not."

The words were spoken flatly, with absolutely no hint of feeling, but Hank took one look at Ann's expression and realized that a whole world of emotion was behind them. In the depths of her eyes he saw stark evidence of feelings he couldn't possibly begin to comprehend. Abandonment. Hurt. Betrayal. Had they been her own? Or had she just seen too much in her life, too many innocent children wronged, too many hearts trampled on? Being a psychologist might equip her with a depth of understanding of human foibles, but the nonstop listening and advising had to take its toll. As he watched, she visibly withdrew, gathering her strength, shrouding her vulnerabilities.

The ease with which she did it saddened him. For a fraction of a second Hank wanted to take the tall, stoic woman in his arms. He wanted to comfort her. He wanted to challenge her easy acceptance of the fact that he was here today, but very likely gone tomorrow. He wanted to promise her a life filled with warmth and love and commitment. He wanted to tell her that the world really wasn't such a lousy place. Ironically, he wasn't sure he believed that himself. Maybe, in the end, he and Ann Davies were two of a kind, both too cynical to believe in happily ever after.

So he didn't argue. He didn't hold her. He didn't do a damn thing, except what he did best: he ran. He turned away from her emotional needs and tackled the practical ones. He went to work on the drain again.

After several minutes of thick, increasingly awkward silence, she left the room. Hank didn't look up. He said nothing.

When she'd gone, the faintest scent of strawberries lingered. It taunted his senses in a way that expensive French perfumes never had. He wondered if the taste of strawberries was on her lips. The possibility was provocative. Maddening. He had the oddest feeling, now that she was out of reach, that he'd made a terrible mistake in not acting on impulse and kissing the woman senseless. Maybe once he'd done it, her odd grip on him would loosen.

His hand slipped and his knuckles scraped along the jagged inside edge of the drain. He cursed as blood welled slowly. He ransacked the medicine cabinet for antiseptic and dumped it on, grateful for the pain. For an instant, anyway, it blocked out his unexpected, inexplicable sense of loss.

It was going to be a very long couple of months.

It was a very long evening. There was absolutely no gracious way Hank could think of to get out of joining the whole unorthodox, noisy family for dinner on his very first night. He figured it was a test contrived by an irritated Maker. He barely passed. His nerves were so tightly wound by the time they finished saying grace and passed the heaping platters of food that his shoulders felt as if he'd been lifting weights for an hour.

He discovered that there was no such thing as conversation, much less seductive intimacy, at a table with six children. There were pokes. There were grumbled complaints about vegetables. There were muttered gripes about the choice of baked rather than fried chicken. There were threats of banishment if one single spoonful of mashed potatoes was actually flung across the table. There were promises of dessert for those who finished their glazed carrots. And there was intense bargaining over dishwashing duties. Ann presided over it all with Madonna-like serenity.

Hank watched her and marveled. While his muscles knotted at the confusion, she seemed to thrive on it. Her cheeks glowed. Her blue eyes sparkled with laughter. She was as adept as an experienced referee in the midst of a goal-line pileup. She knew exactly what everyone needed at any given second and provided it.

Platters and bowls came and went with the precision of a banquet caterer. No argument was allowed to erupt into anger. She teased. She soothed. She tolerated spilled milk and gravy stains with equanimity, but drew the line at food fights.

"Enough," she said, unable to hide a grin as David—or was it Jason? Nope, Jason was the one who never talked—promised to stuff cold potatoes down Tracy's throat if she dared to reveal some secret he'd entrusted her with. Ann moved the potatoes safely out of reach.

"You are such a jerk," Tracy countered with a look of supreme disgust for the red-haired boy beside her. "Why would I want to tell anyone that you—"

"Tracy!" he threatened, stretching to try to get a grip on the bowl that Ann had just moved. An embarrassed flush spread beneath his freckles.

Tracy grinned back. "Gotcha."

"Mom, make her promise," David implored.

"Not me," Ann said, getting up and beginning to clear the table. "You two work it out or leave the table."

David moved his chair with a thump. Tracy propped her elbow on the table and settled her chin in her hand. Her expression of exaggerated innocence amused Hank. He waited for David's next move.

"What'll it cost me?" he said resignedly, sinking back in his chair.

Tracy reacted indignantly. "I am not blackmailing you, you little twerp. Jeez, what's wrong with you? I was only teasing."

Ann paused behind Tracy's chair and put a warning hand on her shoulder. Hank watched as the girl struggled with her anger. "I'm sorry," she muttered finally.

David blinked at the apology, then stared at the table. "Yeah, me, too," he mumbled.

"Now how about dessert?" Ann said cheerfully, ending the brief moment of tension. "Who wants strawberries with ice cream?"

"Me."

"Me."

The chorus came from around the table. Hank found himself chiming in, though the thought of strawberries brought all sorts of dangerous memories to mind. "I'll help," he said, feeling a sudden need to move, a surprising desire to be an active participant, rather than an observer.

"Not tonight," Ann said, her gaze pinning him where he was.

"You told me everyone helped," he reminded her, wondering if this was yet another attempt to set him apart, to remind him that he wasn't a permanent fixture.

She grinned. "We have another rule. No one helps on the first night here."

"Yeah, but after tonight, watch out," Jason warned in a sullen tone. They were the only words he'd spoken since the start of the meal. "Mom's schedules make the army look like summer camp."

"Who'd like Jason's share of dessert?" Ann queried lightly.

Though he'd been slouched down in his chair, feigning disinterest, Jason immediately scrambled to his feet and reached for the bowl.

"Hey, hand it over."

A grin on her face, Ann held the bowl just beyond his reach. Wiry and swift, he tried to grab it, but she made a move as smooth as any Magic Johnson could have performed and passed it over to David at the table. Jason didn't waste time bemoaning the loss. He simply nabbed the one remaining bowl on the counter, and clutching it securely to his chest, went back to his place at the table. The lightening of his mood surprised Hank.

"That's mine," Ann said.

"Oh, really," Jason said with exaggerated innocence.

"Give that back this minute."

"Gee, Mom, are you sure you should be eating all this rich food? There's gotta be cholesterol in this stuff, right? We wouldn't want to watch you die of clogged arteries or something," he said in a way that brought a laugh bubbling up from deep inside Hank. She glared at the two of them, though he was sure he detected a hint of delight as she watched Jason interacting like the rest of them.

"It's really frozen yogurt," she admitted with a look of supreme satisfaction.

"Oh, yuck." David groaned.

"What do you mean, 'oh, yuck'?" Ann retorted. "You ate every bit of it."

"I wouldn't have, if I'd known."

"Which is exactly why I didn't tell you. Next time I take you all out for frozen yogurt, I expect a few less protests." She scowled at Hank and Jason, who were still laughing. "As for you guys, tomorrow the two of you are on KP and I expect something healthier than hot dogs."

"Hamburgers," Hank suggested hopefully.

She gave him a wilting look that relegated hamburgers to the same junk heap that contained corn curls and potato chips.

"I will not fix steamed vegetables," Hank said staunchly.

That drew a chorus of cheers. He turned to Jason and said impulsively, "Think we can catch some fish tomorrow?"

Jason regarded him hesitantly, his brown eyes suddenly hooded and suspicious. There was an instant's tension before he finally said, "Yeah, I guess."

Ann ignored the hesitation and regarded the two of them with pointed skepticism, then turned to Tracy. "If they're not back here with the fish by five-thirty, you might defrost that chicken in the freezer."

"Oh, ye of little faith," Hank said.

"I'd be delighted to have you prove me wrong," she retorted cheerfully as she began clearing the dessert plates.

Hank felt his blood stir at the challenge in her voice and the look in her eyes. It was a look that taunted and teased like a delicate spring breeze. No other woman should dare a look like that unless she meant it, but Hank knew beyond a shadow of a doubt that Ann didn't. In fact, he seriously questioned whether she was even aware of its effect on him. He'd never met a woman less interested in using her femininity to lure a man.

Acting on an irresistible impulse, his arm circled her waist and he pulled her down until their eyes were even. Hers were startled and definitely wary.

"You're playing with fire, lady," he warned in a low voice, not meant to be overheard, though of course it was. He released her slowly, watching as the color heightened in her cheeks, enjoying the sudden, sharp catch of her breath as giggles erupted around the table.

And, then, he felt like a heel. The woman had done nothing but welcome him into her home, and here he was blatantly taunting her right smack in front of her family. He was deliberately trying to seduce her, when he knew perfectly well they were about as suited as a porcupine and an armadillo. When would he learn that not every challenge had to be taken, not every bet won? When, he thought in disgust, would he learn to walk away before someone got hurt?

This time, he promised, glancing around at six expectant young faces. Definitely this time.

Then he made the mistake of looking into those blue, blue eyes again and his pulse ran wild. Common sense and decency fled, chased by something much more primitive.

Oh, hell. Maybe not this time after all.

Chapter Three

As exhausted as if she'd never once closed her eyes, Ann dragged herself out of bed when the alarm went off at six and stumbled into the bathroom. Bleary-eyed, she stared at her pale reflection in the merciless mirror. She looked like hell and felt ten times worse. What was wrong with her? She usually enjoyed getting up early. It gave her an hour to herself before the house filled with noise and her day became guided by other people's demands. Today, though, she felt like crawling back into bed, pulling the covers up over her head and staying there until Hank Riley moved out. Unfortunately that was impossible.

Splashing ice-cold water on her face revived her somewhat. She ran her fingers through her hair in lieu of combing it, then pulled on a pair of running shorts and a shapeless sweatshirt. When she'd added her socks and sneakers, she wandered into the kitchen, put the decaf into the coffee maker and then began a series of warm-up and stretching exercises. She groaned with every single stretch.

Her body was tight as a drum, probably due entirely to the tension set off by that look in Hank's eyes when he'd wrapped his muscular arm around her waist and deliberately taunted her at dinner the night before. Most men did not look at her as if she were a tasty morsel of prime rib and they'd been on a starvation diet. Knowing that Hank probably never looked at any woman in any other way didn't seem to stop the palpitations.

A long, strenuous run was just what she needed to take her mind off the man's invasion of her home. She stepped outside and took a deep, reviving breath of the salty air. The sun was just beginning to lift over the edge of the horizon. It would be another hour before it began to burn off the morning fog. For now it was like being all alone in the world. A sense of peacefulness stole over her.

"You're up early." Hank's voice, low and seductive, emerged eerily from the mist. Ann's just-loosened muscles immediately went taut again. She just barely resisted the desire to curse.

"I'm going running," she replied briskly instead, stepping off the porch. Waving in the general direction of the house, she added, "Help yourself to whatever you want for breakfast, if you don't have time to wait for the rest of us."

She took off at a slow jog. Instead of taking the hint, however, Hank fell into step beside her. She heard the clank of a can as he tossed it in the direction of the porch. Soda? For breakfast? Good God, the man would be dead before his fortieth birthday.

"Mind if I join you?" he asked.

"Would it matter if I did?"

"It might. Try me."

"Stay," she ordered as authoritatively as if he were a resistant puppy. He'd obviously had no obedience training. He stayed right beside her.

"I guess that answers that," she said with a sigh. She glanced sideways and noted that he was wearing a University of Miami Hurricanes sweatshirt that had clearly been through several seasons. The neckline had been stretched, the sleeves cut out. His cutoff jeans revealed powerful legs, corded with muscles. For a man who ate garbage, he looked awfully solid. And strong. And tempting. She dragged her gaze away.

"How far do you usually run?" Hank asked.

"Five miles."

He uttered a choking sound. Ann grinned. Despite his awesome physique, she doubted if Hank Riley ever ran farther than the corner grocery to grab another six-pack. She deliberately picked up her pace. He easily lengthened his stride to match hers.

"Do you do this every morning?" he asked.

"Just about."

"Ever do a marathon?"

"I used to. Now I don't have the time to train properly."

Hank muttered something that sounded like, "Thank God."

"What about you?"

"I don't run," he said, confirming her suspicion. She figured that gave him maybe another mile before he started huffing and puffing.

"I do work out at the gym every day, though," he said, sending her hopes plummeting. "I was going to look for a place down here, but maybe I'll just go running with you instead. I hate to exercise alone, don't you?"

Actually Ann had always considered the solitude the height of heaven. To declare that now, though, would only lead to all sorts of speculation on Hank's part. She could tell he was grinning at her. She glanced over. Yep, the smirk was in place all right. There was also a disconcerting gleam in his eyes as he surveyed her from head to toe, lingering an unnecessarily long time on her bare legs.

"You have great legs," he observed with the authoritative tone of a connoisseur.

Ann could feel the heat begin to rise and it had nothing to do with the exercise. If he expected her to thank him for the sexist compliment, he could wait from now till she won the Boston Marathon.

"Why do you always cover them up with those long skirts?" he persisted.

She frowned at the implied criticism. "I happen to like long skirts."

"Why?"

"Do I need to have a reason?"

"In the overall scheme of life, probably not. As a psychologist, though, I'd think you'd be a little curious about your motivations."

"Long skirts are comfortable."

"And concealing."

"I am not trying to conceal anything," she said adamantly.

"I hope not. With legs like yours . . ."

"I do not want to talk about my legs."

"So it does make you uncomfortable when men find them attractive?"

"It does not!"

He was laughing at her again. "I thought so," he said with that infuriatingly self-satisfied tone that made her want to rip the hairs of his beard out one by one.

Ann finished her run ten minutes faster than usual. She'd run, in fact, as though she were being chased by the devil himself. All in all, she figured it was an apt analogy.

Hank was late. In fact, he'd been running late ever since he'd gone jogging with Ann. He'd skipped breakfast to try to catch up, but that lost half hour in the morning plagued him the rest of the day.

It had been worth it, though. The discovery that the woman had an absolutely knockout body under all those layers of clothes had practically taken his breath away. He hadn't been able to get the image of those slender, well-shaped legs, the smooth white skin and the subtle bounce of her breasts out of his mind. He'd lost a good ten minutes of every hour daydreaming about her. He'd wasted another five cursing himself because of it.

Now he was running behind for his fishing date with Jason. He'd promised to meet him at four, but at three-thirty the construction crew started balking over the quality of some of the materials that had been delivered that morning. Hank went with them to check up on the complaints and found they were valid. The materials were obviously an inferior grade. Whether it was a simple mistake or an outright attempt to defraud the company, it meant a waste of time and money to correct. Had it not been caught, it could have been disastrous down the line. It was the sort of corner cutting he and Todd had never tolerated on one of their jobs.

Furious, he spent the next hour on the phone trying to reach the supplier, whose secretary was amazingly adept at evasion. No doubt she'd had a lot of practice. He slammed the phone down for the fifth time, then glanced at the clock. It was already four-thirty. He picked up the phone again and called Miami, this time for Todd.

"Do me a favor, would you, and see if you can straighten this mess out," he requested when he reached his partner.

"I'll try, but you've dealt with this guy before. Can't you get anywhere with him?"

"I might be able to if I spent the next hour hanging around waiting for him to get back to me, but I have an appointment."

"One that's more important than this?"

Hank hesitated. He could understand Todd's amazement. In all the years they'd known each other, Hank had never walked out in the middle of a fight. He actually enjoyed sparring with the more difficult personalities.

Before he could think of an adequate response, Todd demanded, "Okay, buddy, what's up down there?"

Hank evaded. "Nothing."

"Let me guess. You've got a heavy date at five in the afternoon."

"Not exactly," he mumbled. He was used to the teasing about his active social life, but today it made him even more irritable than usual. He'd have hung up if he hadn't known that Todd would only call back with more amused taunts. As a recently reformed ladies' man himself, Todd's wit could be particularly barbed and uncannily accurate.

"What, then?" he was asking now.

"I'm going fishing."

Todd's hoot of laughter could have been heard clear to Marathon without benefit of the phone line. Hank bristled. "What's so damn funny about that?" he growled.

"The last time you went fishing, you got seasick. You swore you'd never go near a boat again unless it was the size of the biggest liner in Carnival's fleet."

"I'm not going in a boat. I'm going to stand on a dock."

"Ah-ha," Todd said slowly. "It's all beginning to make sense. As I recall, Ann loves to fish. Did she talk you into this?"

"Why would you think that?"

"Because you would never decide to spend the evening this way on your own, but with a woman involved, now that's another story entirely."

"Actually, it was not Ann's idea. Not exactly anyway. I'm in charge of dinner tonight. Since she turned down hamburger and we had chicken last night, that left fish and if I don't get out of here in the next ten minutes, it's going to be too dark for me to see to bait the damn hook."

"You could stop at the fish market."

"It wouldn't be the same. Besides, I promised Jason."

"Jason?"

"One of the kids."

"I see. Sounds domestic."

"Cut it out, Todd. Will you call the supplier back or not?"

"I'll call him."

"Thanks."

"Hank?"

"Yes?"

"The fish market's right on the highway. You can't miss it."

"Go to hell, buddy." He slammed the phone down on another hoot of laughter. He was still muttering about Todd's uncalled-for glee when he pulled into the driveway at the house. Tracy was sitting on the steps watching Tommy and Melissa play on the swings that hung from the branches of the banyan tree.

"You're late," she announced.

"I know. Where's Jason?"

She shrugged. "He got tired of waiting."

"Damn." For some reason, Jason's attitude the night before had made him nervous. He'd been counting on this time alone with him to see if his uneasiness was justified.

"He took a fishing pole with him, though. Try across the street. There's a dock over there."

"Any more poles around here?"

"Ann's is by the kitchen door. Right over there," she said, pointing behind her.

"Thanks." He found the pole and was halfway around the house when he looked back and saw Tracy staring dejectedly at the ground. He realized then that she'd looked just as down when he'd driven up. With Ann not due home for quite a while, he couldn't bring himself to walk off and leave her that way.

He came back, dug around in the tackle box for a minute and asked casually, "You okay?"

She glanced up, looking surprised by the question. Then her gaze shifted down again. "Yeah, sure."

"No school today?"

"Yeah. I went."

There was an odd, flat note in her voice. He couldn't quite recognize it, but it disturbed him. He sat down beside her. Uncomfortable at being cast in the role of confidant, he searched for the right question to ask a sensitive teenager who was practically a stranger. He opted for being direct. "Did something happen?"

She shook her head. "Not really."

He recognized the evasion. "Which means something did, but you don't want to talk about it?"

That drew a slight smile. "I guess."

"Okay, fair enough," he said, respecting her need for privacy, even though her mood worried him. "Sometimes things don't seem quite so awful once you've talked them out. Keep that in mind, okay? Ann's a pretty good listener from all I hear and I'm willing to give it a shot, too, if you need somebody as a sounding board.''

"Okay. Thanks.''

Reluctant to leave her and still hoping that she might unburden herself, he sat there for another couple of minutes watching as Paul came racing out of the house and started shooting baskets. David hovered in the doorway.

"Hey, David,'' he called out. "Why don't you get out there and challenge him? I'll bet you're every bit as good at basketball as he is.''

David shook his head.

"He doesn't play much,'' Tracy explained. "Ann says it's because he got kicked out of so many foster homes for being too much trouble. He was always getting hurt and stuff.''

Hank was shocked. "But that's what boys do.''

"I know, but some foster parents don't want to be bothered. Now I guess he's scared Ann will make him leave, too.''

"That's...'' He couldn't even think of a word to describe an adult who'd beat down a child's spirit that way.

"Awful,'' Tracy supplied. "I know. Sometimes Jason can get him to do stuff, but most of the time he doesn't bother, either. Ann figures we just have to keep trying. Sooner or later David's gonna realize that it's different here.''

Hank's respect for the challenges Ann faced with these kids increased tenfold as he studied the wistful expression on David's face. His heart ached for him. While he was trying to figure out if there was something he could do, Tracy cast a sidelong look at him. "You'd better go catch those fish. Ann will be home soon. She'll never let you forget it if she has to cook that chicken tonight."

Reluctantly he got to his feet. "Never fear," he said, then leaned down to whisper, "I know where the fish market is."

Tracy giggled at that and, for an instant anyway, her somber expression vanished, replaced by that glorious smile that would turn her into a heartbreaker in another couple of years. An unfamiliar stirring of tenderness welled up inside him and he got the first inkling why some adults got so hooked on parenting. It was the first time he'd experienced the impact that youthful, carefree laughter could have on a jaded heart.

The water was calmer on the gulf side of the key. The setting sun was hovering at the edge of the horizon, a huge orange ball ready to dip below the endless sea of blue. Already there was a chill in the air, which made Hank glad he'd thought to grab his jacket from the truck on the way over. When he spotted Jason, however, the teenager was huddled at the end of the dock wearing jeans and a T-shirt. He could practically see the goose bumps standing out on his skinny arms.

Hank walked to the end of the dock and put down his gear. Jason didn't acknowledge his presence with so much as a glance. Only a slight stiffening of his shoulders indicated that he was even aware that Hank had joined him.

"Catch anything?" Hank asked.

Jason said nothing.

"Sorry I'm late. I got held up at work."

The apology was met with silence. Hank's earlier feelings of guilt were rapidly changing to impatience. "Jason, I'm talking to you."

The boy turned a sullen gaze on him. "So?"

"I expect you to answer me."

"Why should I?"

"Because it's polite."

"It's polite to keep your promises, too. Ain't that right?"

Hank held on to his temper. He recalled what Ann had said about these kids having been mistreated by far too many adults along the way. "Yes, that is right. I've explained, though. I am sorry I got held up."

"Right." He sounded skeptical and angry. Years of rejection had obviously taken their toll.

Hank tried again with a more neutral topic. "I understand I'm borrowing your room."

"It's Mom's house. She can do what she wants."

"But it's your room and I appreciate your letting me use it. I like the posters."

Jason ignored him. Hank had no idea what else to say in the face of all that pent-up hostility, so they sat on the dock in silence until Jason reeled in a good-size snapper.

"That's a beauty," Hank said. Jason almost managed a smile as he unhooked the fish and plopped it into a bucket of seawater. "You're good at this."

Jason shrugged, dismissing the success. "There's not much to it."

"I don't know about that. I haven't caught anything yet."

After another instant of suspicious silence, Jason suggested grudgingly, "Maybe it's your bait. What'd you bring?"

"Shrimp."

"That should be good."

"You fish a lot?"

"Some."

"Who taught you?"

"I just did it. All the guys in Key West did."

"That's where you're from? Key West?"

Jason nodded, then said, "Why don't you just say what's on your mind?"

"What?"

"Don't you want to know how I got here?"

Hank knew at once he was treading on treacherous ground. As he had earlier with Tracy, he felt out of his depth. "If you want to tell me," he said finally.

"I was in jail," Jason said bluntly. His expression was defiant, daring Hank to react badly.

"Mom bailed me out," Jason added. "Then she brought me here."

Hank had to swallow his shock. He didn't want Jason to see how troubled he was by his belligerent announcement. Was Ann out of her mind, though? What on earth had possessed her to take in some kid who was in trouble with the law?

"What did you do?"

Jason glared at him. "Who says I did anything?"

"There usually aren't too many innocent people in jail, at least not for long."

"Okay, so maybe you're right."

"And?"

"I stole a car. So what? It was no big deal."

"Grand theft sounds like a big deal to me. Why'd you do it?"

"I needed to get to the store."

His sarcasm set Hank's teeth on edge. Again he swallowed his irritation and repeated, "Why'd you do it?"

"My old man needed the money."

The flat tone sent a chill through Hank. "Bad enough to make you steal?"

"When you need a fix bad enough, you don't worry about how you get it. It wasn't the first thing I did. It was just the first time I got caught." Jason made it sound as though *that* were the crime.

Hank felt his stomach churn. Anger and pity welled up deep inside him. "What you did was wrong," he reminded Jason.

Jason regarded him defiantly, then retorted with youthful bitterness, "Where I come from you're taught to mind your parents."

Hank could see the twisted logic at work. What worried him, though, was how much it was still affecting Jason's thinking. Was the boy ready to break the law again at any provocation? What kind of influence could he possibly be on all those other kids Ann had taken under her wing? He tried telling himself it was none of his business. He tried telling himself she'd be furious at his meddling. He looked again at the tense, angry kid beside him and decided he had no choice. There was no way in hell he could remain uninvolved. He would talk to Ann the minute they were alone.

Getting Ann alone, however, was no easy task with six children underfoot. It was after nine by the time the little ones were in bed and the older kids were settled down doing their homework. Hank took a beer from the refrigerator, popped it open and held it out toward Ann. She shook her head.

"You want something else?"

"No."

"Feel like taking a walk by the water? It's a nice night."

She regarded him warily. Hank grinned. "Don't panic. I'm not planning to rip off your clothes and have my way with you."

Ironically, as soon as the denial was out of his mouth, Hank realized it was a blatant lie. He did want to strip away the layered T-shirts, the too-long skirt and those ridiculous socks. Those socks were orange tonight. With a blue skirt and yellow and green shirts. She reminded him of a particularly colorful parrot.

She also smelled like strawberries again, which made him want to taste the creamy white skin of her neck. Which made him achingly hard. Which would have made the lie obvious if she'd looked anywhere other than straight past him as she said stiffly, "I never thought you were."

Hank held the screen door open. As she marched past him, he wondered what perversity made him want a woman who was all sharp angles and tart tongue, a woman who clearly regarded him as a nuisance. There were a dozen other less complicated women he could have called for a date. Unfortunately, the only woman he seemed interested in spending time with tonight was this one.

They walked in silence. It was Ann who finally broke it.

"Was there something you wanted to talk about?"

"Can't a man just enjoy the night and your charming company without wanting something?"

She regarded him skeptically. "It's possible, but you don't strike me as the type."

"How do I strike you?" he asked, suddenly curious about her impression. She was a psychologist. The possibility that she might be able to read between the lines and detect things about him that even he didn't admit was troublesome.

"As a man used to getting what he wants, women included."

He laughed, relieved. There were no uncanny revelations in that analysis. "I can't deny that. Is there something wrong with going after the things that are important to you? Isn't that what life is all about?"

"It depends on who gets trampled in the process."

"Do you think I'm trying to trample on you, Annie?"

"You've only been here two days."

"Exactly." He grinned. "And I've been on my best behavior."

"Why doesn't that reassure me?"

"You're the psychologist. You tell me."

She suddenly hugged her arms protectively around her waist. Hank had an urgent desire to push them away, to draw them around his own waist so that he could feel her slender body pressed into his. He figured she'd slug him if he tried. He decided he'd better change the subject.

"I wanted to talk to you about Jason."

Her gaze shot to his, her nervousness apparent. "What about him?"

"I think you're taking a bad risk having him here."

She stopped in midstep and her hands went at once to her hips. Challenging. Defiant. Mother-hen protective. "Why on earth would you say something like that? You don't even know him."

"Simmer down," he soothed. "I know he's had problems with the police. He doesn't seem especially remorseful about it, either."

Her expression changed to one of astonishment. "He told you that?"

"More or less."

Her face lit up as if he'd just announced that the kid had been accepted at Harvard. "Don't you see how wonderful that is?"

"Wonderful? It was scary sitting there with this skinny kid talking about stealing cars and taking dope as if it were perfectly ordinary stuff."

"In his life, it was."

"And that's the kind of influence you want around the others?"

"Jason doesn't try to influence the others. He practically says nothing at all. The fact that he opened up to you means he's beginning to trust adults again. He was obviously anxious for your approval."

"It sounded to me more like bragging. I think he was more interested in shocking me. The boy could be dangerous."

She waved off his fears. "He's not dangerous. He's scared."

Deep in his gut Hank wanted to believe Ann was right. He'd seen for himself the evidence of vulnerable kid behind the tough, grown-up facade. He'd known a lot of kids just like that in his time. Some of them grew up and made something of themselves. Some of them didn't. Those were the ones who scared the hell out of him. He reached out and gently touched Ann's uptilted chin. "What if you're wrong?" he asked gently.

"I am not wrong," she said stubbornly. "With the right environment, the right sort of support and a little unconditional love, Jason will do just fine."

He sighed with impatience at the Pollyanna viewpoint. "You're too trusting, Annie."

"And you're too cynical."

"Being a liberal do-gooder is just fine, as long as it doesn't endanger anyone else."

"I'd rather be a liberal do-gooder than a self-centered jerk."

"It is not self-centered to worry about you and those kids," he retorted angrily, though he was surprised himself at the depth of his concern. That she dismissed his fears so lightly made him indignant. The fact that he wanted her anyway stunned him. His blood pounded. When Ann parted her lips to counter his last furious comment, he settled his mouth over hers. It was the only way he could think of to silence her.

It was also the only way he could think of to still the demanding throb that had his entire body quivering with the irrational, uncontrollable need to know her touch. He expected a fight, perhaps even hoped for one to prove how foolish the attraction was. Instead her lips were velvet soft and trembling beneath his. And, after an instant's startled stiffening, she relaxed against him. Her arms drifted around his neck. Her hips tilted into his, a perfect fit. Pleasure shot through him. Hot, searing desire replaced casual curiosity.

And Hank knew he was in more trouble than Jason had ever dreamed of.

Chapter Four

Ann heard the music the instant she turned into the driveway. Beethoven? At full blast? She had to be hearing things. She was used to being greeted by rock and roll at best. She listened more closely. The familiar classical strains swelled, carrying on the turbulent wind. It was definitely Beethoven. The night air was suddenly filled with violins and the sound of waves crashing against the shore. She felt as if she'd stumbled into the midst of an outdoor concert in which man and nature combined to stir the soul.

Exhausted and drained by a nerve-racking series of sessions, to say nothing of the residual impact of Hank Riley's totally unexpected and thoroughly devastating kiss the previous night, she leaned back in the front seat of the car. The music flowed over her, soothing, working its magic. Her eyes drifted closed. Hank's provocative image appeared at once. She opened her eyes to banish him, but the image lingered just as plainly. She gave up the pointless battle and shut her eyes again. Her lips curved in a smile at the pleasantly surprising sensation of peace after so many hours of jarring dissonance.

"Annie?"

Dazed, she blinked at the sound of Hank's voice.

"You okay?" he asked, leaning down beside the car and peering in at her. His blue eyes were filled with tender concern. Recognizing it, her heart tapped a new and surprisingly sensual rhythm. It had been years since anyone had ever worried about her, even fleetingly. She was the strong, clear-thinking one. She was the one others came to to pour out their troubles. Whether privately or professionally, she was expected to cope, to endure. The fact that this man thought she might occasionally need help in doing that made her feel cherished somehow, even as it sometimes irritated her. *Sometimes?* It almost always irritated her. But not tonight. Tonight she basked in the unfamiliar warmth of the sensation.

"I'm fine," she told him now. "I was just enjoying the concert."

He grinned ruefully. "Sorry if it was too loud. The kids haven't complained, so I didn't realize how far the sound carried."

"Don't apologize. It was wonderful to come home to that. Just what I needed."

"Bad day?"

"No worse than most others. I just seemed to have less patience with it." Probably because she'd been up half the night for the second night in a row trying to make sense of the astonishing effect this man had on her. Her entire body—and her common sense—had melted in his arms. She hadn't been able to come up with a single, logical explanation for it and she was a woman addicted to logic. Logic made sense of life, brought order out of chaos. And it was tidier by far than being prey to erratic emotions. Even though she knew all that, she looked into his eyes and felt the irrational tug of desire starting all over again.

"Have you eaten?" he said.

She shook her head.

"Then come sit on the porch and let me bring you something. Tracy made vegetable soup. With this chill in the air, it seemed like a good night for it."

Beethoven? Homemade soup? What was going on here? "Who's idea was all this?"

"All what?"

"The music and the soup."

"Tracy had the recipe book out and the soup on when I came in from work. She said something about experimenting. It sounded dangerous to me, but it turned out to be edible. Paul and David actually finished every bite. Melissa picked out all the carrots and Tommy threw them across the room, but I think we found the last of them. It's safe to come in now."

She regarded him oddly. He actually sounded as though he'd enjoyed the evening. He was adapting far more readily than she'd anticipated. It sounded as though the children were, too. That pleased her, even as it made her uneasy. How long would it last? How long before he vanished from their lives?

"After all that," he was saying, "I felt like listening to some music. I hope you don't mind that I went through your CDs."

"Not at all. I must admit I'm a little surprised by your choice."

He turned a knowing grin on her. "I'm sure you expected a preference for twanging guitars over violin concertos."

"Something like that," she conceded.

"Loretta Lynn and Tammy Wynette have their places. So do Beethoven and Mozart. I'll have you know I can even manage a little Chopin on the piano."

"You?"

"Three years of piano lessons," he boasted.

"Your mother must have been very strong-willed to manage that."

"My mother had nothing to do with it," he said with an unmistakable edge in his voice. "I took the lessons a few years ago."

Intrigued by his tone, she was more astounded by his announcement. She stared at him in wonder. "You took piano lessons when you were—"

"Thirty-four," he supplied, chuckling as he held up hands that looked far too large, far too strong, to be used in such a gentle pursuit. Those hands playing Chopin? Those hands caressing...

She brought herself up short just as he said, "Hard to imagine, isn't it? I'd always wanted to play, though. There was no money for lessons when I was a kid. Besides, I probably would have been laughed off the football team. At thirty-four I had no excuses left."

"Good for you."

He winked at her. "Be careful, Annie. You may just discover that I'm full of surprises."

Her pulse skipped at the teasing challenge in his voice. All at once she recalled every second that she'd spent in his arms, every sensation that had been aroused by his lips on hers. There was a subtle stirring low in her abdomen. An irrational yearning filled her heart. Wild, magical nights like this were meant to be shared with someone special and she'd been alone far too long. Why couldn't she put aside her doubts and her tendency to analyze things to death? When had she stopped taking risks and turned her life into a predictable routine or as predictable as any life could be with children around? Why couldn't she accept for just this one night the possibility that Hank Riley could be that someone, that he wasn't just an impertinent rogue on the make, that he genuinely cared about her?

Her gaze met his, caught and held. Hers was tentative. His was daring and bold, almost hypnotic in its unwavering intensity. Without taking his eyes from hers, he slowly opened the car door and waited for her to step out. He left just enough room for her to exit without touching him—if she chose. Heart thudding in her chest, she stood, but she couldn't bring herself to take the one tiny step that would put her back into his arms for another of those inhibition-melting kisses. She wanted to. Dear Lord, how she wanted to. But tonight years of restraint and common sense held her back.

Hank's smile was slow and gentle and knowing. "It'll happen, Annie," he promised in a low voice that sizzled down her spine. "Count on it."

The vow eased her instant of regret. It also set her blood on fire in a way she'd never dreamed possible. Trembling, she brushed past him and went inside. She fumbled with the ladle for the soup until Hank finally took it from her and poured a steaming bowlful. He put it in front of her at the table, touched her shoulder with tantalizing tenderness and then he left her to her thoughts.

They were in turmoil.

It was the damn Beethoven, she told herself. And the Chopin.

It was the kiss, she finally confessed with more honesty. One stupid, meaningless kiss and the man had her feeling like a teenager whose hormones were newly rampaging out of control. She'd taken enough courses, handled enough cases to recognize good old-fashioned lust when it hit her in the gut. Forget his tenderness. Forget the concern. What she was feeling had nothing to do with those gentler qualities. What she was feeling was heart-tumbling, spine-tingling desire for the man's body. Recognizing it was half the battle. Now all she had to do was ignore it and sooner or later it would wear off.

Or cause her to do something incredibly stupid. The list of possibilities there was enough to make her choke on her soup. It began with falling into bed with him. It ended with falling in love.

"It'll never happen," she muttered adamantly.

"What won't happen?" Hank inquired curiously.

Her gaze shot up. He was standing in the doorway, watching her again, Melissa cradled contentedly against his shoulder. How could a man the size of a truck move so stealthily? Maybe she ought to insist he wear a bell around his neck. She could use the warning in order to get her defenses into place. Right now he was probably seeing naked longing in her eyes. Terrific, she thought with disgust. Just great!

"Hi," Melissa said with a sleepy smile. She held out her arms. Ann took her.

"Did you have a good day, pumpkin?"

Melissa nodded. "Hank and me builded a sand castle. Wanna see?"

"It's a little dark to see it now. We'll look in the morning."

"Hanks says it'll be all gone by then." She gave him a beguiling grin. "We do it again, okay?"

He laughed. "Okay, squirt. Now remember what we talked about."

She nodded. "I go to bed now."

"That's right. Ann will come tuck you in."

"You, too?"

"Me, too."

"Okay."

When she had toddled off, Hank pulled out a chair, turned it around and sat down straddling it.

"I never thought I'd see the day," he said, his eyes filled with amusement.

"What's that supposed to mean?" she said.

"You, tongue-tied. Makes me wonder what you really were thinking about when Melissa and I arrived."

"A case," she improvised hastily. "It's a tough one. It really has me stymied."

"Oh, really."

"Yes. This couple, they, um, they can't seem to figure out what they want."

He looked immediately interested. "So, what'd you tell 'em?"

Gathering her defenses, she met his gaze evenly. "I told them if they couldn't make up their minds about each other, then getting together was probably the wrong decision."

"But aren't doubts normal, especially when a relationship is new?"

"Some doubts, yes. But if the love's not powerful enough to overshadow them, then perhaps it's not strong enough to survive, either."

"Perhaps," he echoed, reaching out to pick her hand up off the table. His thumb rubbed across her knuckles. "No guarantees?"

Ann felt an incredible tension begin to build inside just from the brush of his callused thumb across her hand. Her voice was shaky when she said, "There are never any guarantees, with or without doubts."

He turned her hand over, lifted it up and kissed the palm. A current of electricity jolted through her as he said solemnly, "So you might as well play the hand out and see where it leads, right?"

She shook her head and nervously snatched her hand away. "Sometimes it's better just to cut your losses."

"When?" He asked the question very seriously, but she caught the desire to laugh lurking in his eyes.

She swallowed hard and tried to think straight. "When what?"

"When do you know it's time to cut your losses?"

Now, she wanted to shout. "That's a very individual sort of thing," she said sensibly, struggling against the emotions sweeping through her, fighting the temptation in his eyes.

"Let's take you and me, for instance."

He made the suggestion in all innocence. Still, her eyes blinked wide. "What?"

"You and me," he repeated. "Purely hypothetical, of course. On the surface, you and I couldn't be more unsuited, right?"

She nodded weakly.

"But we're living here together for the time being and there's this attraction growing between us."

She tried valiantly for indignation. "Attraction?" Her voice was barely above a whisper. Instead of skepticism, however, she merely managed to convey nervousness.

"Sure. Lust. Chemistry. You know what I mean."

"We're talking hypothetical here?"

"Naturally. Now is that something that should be played out to its logical conclusion?"

"Absolutely not," she said in a rush.

"Under no circumstances?"

"None."

"Why?"

"You said it yourself. We're unsuited."

"On the surface."

"That's all we know about each other."

"And we shouldn't bother trying to dig beneath the surface? Maybe there's more we have in common than we realize. Where there's Beethoven, who knows, there could be Wagner."

She was shaking her head. "Definitely not."

"Definitely not Wagner?" he teased. "Or definitely not us?"

"Us," she said, barely getting the word past a throat gone suddenly dry.

He tilted the chair forward and touched his lips to her forehead. "Coward," he murmured softly.

And then, with a wink that made her heart flip over, he was gone again. One of these days, when she had her wits about her, she was going to have to talk to him about walking out in the middle of a conversation. It was a really lousy way to have the last word.

Super Bowl Sunday. Hank could hardly wait. He'd thought about going back to Miami to hang out with the guys, but by the time he'd finished working on Saturday it had been too damn late to tackle the drive. He considered going to a bar, which would be rowdy and filled with eager fans. But as beat as he was, nothing appealed to him more than settling down in front of the TV at home with a six-pack of beer, some chips and maybe a couple of hamburgers at halftime.

He hadn't stopped to consider that Ann would regard the entire plan as tantamount to treason.

"You want to do what?" she said when he suggested they flip the channel on the TV away from some documentary on PBS.

"Watch the game." When she stared at him blankly, he added, "The Super Bowl. You know, the big end-of-the-season matchup. This is what it's all about."

She looked appalled. And unyielding. "Only if you're a cretin," she said emphatically.

He sighed heavily. "Oh, Annie, there were such sad gaps in your education."

"There were no gaps in my education. I have my B.A., my M.A. and my Ph.D."

"But you obviously missed cheerleading."

"Thank God." She said it so fervently he had to hide a smile.

"Now, Annie, how do you expect to identify with your average American male if you know nothing about the sport that consumes most of his Sunday afternoons from August through January? You owe it to yourself and the future of your practice to watch the Super Bowl."

"I prefer to identify with his poor wife, who's left to raise the children, mow the lawn and suffer in silence while the slob sits in front of a TV and stares at a bunch of grown men beating one another's brains out."

"Obviously you've missed the finer points of the game," he said dryly.

"That's okay by me."

This clearly wasn't getting them anywhere. Ann's beliefs seemed entrenched. With only ten minutes to go until game time, he didn't have a lot of time to win her over. He gazed longingly at the comfortable sofa and the twenty-four-inch television screen. "Is there another TV in the house?"

"Jason and Paul have an old black-and-white set in their room."

Hank felt his heartbeat screech to a halt. It would be a travesty to watch the Super Bowl in anything less than color. "I don't suppose . . ."

"Not on your life," she said adamantly, turning the sound back up with a quick flick of the remote control.

If he drove like hell, there was still time to get to a bar. Or he could suffer through the game in black-and-white. Or, he decided with a certain amount of roguish delight, he could use his considerable charms to get Annie to change her mind about sharing the set. As skittish as she was, ten minutes ought to be just enough time for that. He dropped down on the sofa beside her, mere inches from her.

"So what are you watching?"

She regarded him warily. "It's a report on herbal medicine in China."

"Any good?"

"It's fascinating."

"Good. Tell me what's happened so far."

She gave him a sharp look. "Why?"

"So I can catch up. If this is what we're going to watch, I don't want to feel left out."

"This isn't a suspense thriller. You won't be confused if you don't know what's already happened."

"But you said what you'd seen so far was fascinating. Fascinate me."

"I thought you wanted to watch the Super Bowl."

"I did, but I'd rather spend a quiet evening right here with you." He allowed his hand to drift innocently to her thigh when he said it. He felt the muscle jerk beneath his touch, but to her credit Ann never glanced away from the television.

"Go away, Hank."

"Am I bothering you?"

"Yes."

He chuckled at her honest, heartfelt response. She turned a fierce scowl on him.

"Go away," she repeated.

"Why? I think this is cozy. I want to share your interests. If this herbal medicine thing is as good as you say it is, I'm sure I'll enjoy it just as much as a football game."

With a deep sigh, she turned and handed him the remote control. "You win. Watch the game."

"Are you sure?" He'd flipped the channel before the question was out of his mouth.

"Very sure," she said wryly, getting to her feet.

Hank grabbed her wrist and pulled her back down. "Stay and watch it with me."

"When pigs fly."

"Give it a chance. I was willing to watch the China thing with you."

"Sure you were."

"Honest."

She chuckled despite herself. "Your nose is growing, Riley."

"Okay, so it was a calculated risk. Stay and watch this with me. Football's no fun alone." He reached behind the sofa and came up with two beers. "Here you go."

To his astonishment, she took the bottle without protest and tilted it up. When she took another long swallow and then another, he began to get worried. "Maybe you should slow down," he said.

"Why? Isn't this the way you're supposed to watch the game? A beer in one hand, a bowl of chips in the other. Where are the chips, by the way? I'm sure you have them hidden away somewhere."

Still watching her warily, he reached behind the sofa again and retrieved the potato chips.

"Any dip?" she inquired as she took a handful.

"In the refrigerator," he murmured, bemused by her odd behavior. Chips? Dip? Why wasn't she yelling her head off by now? "I'll get it."

When he came back, to his amazement she hadn't switched channels. He held out the onion dip. She loaded down a chip with the sour-cream mixture, then popped it into her mouth.

"Are you okay?"

"Fine."

"But you hate all this stuff."

"But I'm a good sport. Don't forget that. Now be quiet. They're playing the National Anthem."

All through the first quarter, Ann sat stoically beside him, drinking her beer and eating potato chips as if she'd been deprived of them since childhood. She did not, however, look as though she were enjoying herself. She closed her eyes every time she anticipated the players making contact, which meant she was missing most of the game.

She watched the aftermath of a particularly violent third-down defense with a sort of avid fascination, then shivered. "Brutal. What is wrong with you? How can you stand this?" she said, turning her gaze on him. She actually looked shaken.

"Annie, this isn't just a matter of brute force out there. It's not just twenty-two guys trying to see how hard they can slam into one another."

"You'll never prove that to me."

"I can if you'll keep your eyes open for a couple of plays here. Now watch this. See the receiver going out for that pass. See that leap, the way he turns his body and reaches over his shoulder for the ball. Have you ever seen a ballet dancer execute a turn any more gracefully than that?"

"What do you know about ballet?" she scoffed.

"Season ticket holder, Miami City Ballet," he retorted.

She stared in obvious astonishment. "You?"

"Me. Do you know that male dancers have almost as many injuries as football players? They wind up with bad backs, knee surgery, hip replacements. Do you wince when you see them on stage?"

She considered the argument thoughtfully. "I never thought of it like that."

"These men are just as agile in their own way. If you watch a game as an exercise in athletic skill, rather than a display of brute strength, it takes on a whole different perspective."

She glanced at the screen, then back at him. "Ballet, huh?"

"Pirouettes, leaps and all."

"I'll give it another inning."

He groaned. "Half, Annie. Another half."

Chapter Five

The last of Ann's patients had left an hour ago. She'd finished her notes, put away the files, emptied the teapot, cleaned the disgusting ashtrays she permitted only in the waiting room and tidied her desk. She'd even plumped every last cushion on the sofa and aligned every slat in the vertical blinds. Practically the only thing left that could possibly delay her departure for home was kneeling down and picking every piece of lint from the carpet. She glanced down consideringly, then muttered an oath that rarely crossed her lips.

She was losing it. If this wasn't proof enough, then yesterday's behavior was. She had sat in front of the television through an entire football game. She had actually caught herself cheering for one extraordinarily evasive runner. She'd only barely noticed the violent tackles that had cleared his path. She had eaten more than her share of a huge bowl of greasy potato chips slathered with sour-cream-and-onion dip. She'd allowed the kids to order pizzas for dinner. Stunned by the unexpected permission, they had asked for fat-laden pepperoni and sausage. She hadn't even blinked. She blamed it on the beer.

Worse, though she would never on pain of death admit it to another soul, she had enjoyed herself. More precisely, she had enjoyed sharing the evening with Hank. Over the past few days, she had even started looking forward to their morning runs. Now she awoke to coffee already perking and Hank waiting for her on the back porch. The five miles had started to go by all too quickly.

Which was, of course, exactly why she didn't want to go home now. Hank was going to be there. Every sexy, self-confident, increasingly intriguing inch of him. Lord only knew what temptation he had planned for her tonight. He seemed to have established himself as some sort of guiding spirit whose only purpose in life was to make her forget all of her long-held, rational beliefs. He was doing a darn good job of it. He was proof incarnate that opposites attract. She was struggling to keep in mind that it was usually disaster when they did. Maybe a review of a few of her case files would drive home the point.

When the phone rang, she grabbed it, praying for a reprieve from yet another struggle against some perverse fate that had tossed her into this emotional fray.

"Dr. Davies."

"Ann, it's Tom. How'd you like to do your civic duty tonight?"

The mayor! Perfect. The gods were listening after all. She lifted her eyes heavenward and without asking a single question said a fervent, "Yes!"

Tom laughed. "Don't you even want to know what I'm after?"

"Well, of course, but I trust your judgment. It must be important or you wouldn't be asking."

"How come you're never that complimentary when I'm asking for a date?"

"Maybe it has something to do with knowing that I'd be competing with the entire female population of the Keys."

"I'd throw them all over for you."

"You say that, knowing you're safe. If I took you up on it, you'd develop a nervous tic. Now what exactly did you need me to do tonight?"

"There's a hearing in Key West on offshore drilling. Can you go? I'll drive. We need bodies down there."

"No brains?"

"Okay. That goes without saying. What about it?"

"Of course I'll go. Let me call home and make arrangements for the kids."

"Terrific. I'll pick you up at the office in ten minutes. Sorry about the late notice, but we just got word that the state officials were coming tonight. We'd thought it was only a preliminary strategy session."

"No problem. See you soon."

She disconnected the call, then dialed home. Melissa answered. Next to overflowing bathtubs, the telephone was her favorite thing.

"Hi, sweetheart," Ann said.

"Hi." Melissa whispered the response so softly Ann could barely hear her.

"Honey, is Tracy there?"

That was greeted by a long silence, then finally a hesitant, "No."

"How about Jason?"

"Uh-huh."

"Can you get him for me?"

"Okay."

Melissa hung up the phone. Ann gritted her teeth and called back.

"Hi," Melissa said cheerfully.

Ann used her sternest tone, the one that always got results. "Melissa, I want you to get Jason at once."

This time the phone clattered to the floor. She heard Melissa's footsteps receding, accompanied by choking sobs.

"Oh, Lord. Now what?" Tapping her fingers against the desktop, she waited on the off chance that Melissa would actually get Jason. She could hear the shouts of various children in the background.

"Hey," Paul yelled. "Who left the phone off the hook?"

"Paul!" she yelled back, just as the phone clicked off.

She dialed again. This time Paul answered.

"Paul, it's Mom."

"Oh, hi, Mom. Have you been trying to call? The phone's been off the hook."

"I know," she said with rapidly ebbing patience. "Would you please get Jason for me?"

"Sure thing. Hey, Jason, Mom wants to talk to you. Are you coming home soon? Melissa's crying something fierce."

"She'll be okay," Ann promised just as she heard Tom's horn blow. "Is Jason coming?"

"Yeah, he's right here, but I gotta ask you something first. Is it okay if Hank takes Tommy and me to the construction site tonight?"

She couldn't imagine Hank volunteering to do that. "Is that your idea or his?"

"He said it would be okay."

She sighed. "I'm not sure that's an answer, but if he's willing, fine. Be careful, though, and do exactly what he tells you to do."

"Okay," he said quickly. "Here's Jason."

Visions of Tommy tumbling off a girder twenty feet in the sky suddenly made her shake. "Wait, Paul...Paul!"

"It's me, Jason. What's up, Mom?"

"Tell Paul to be sure to hold Tommy's hand the whole time they're at that construction site."

"I'll tell him, but how come you didn't tell him yourself?"

Ann very nearly groaned. "Just tell him, Jason. And tell him to do exactly what Hank says."

"Is that all you wanted?"

"No, it is not all I wanted!" She took a deep breath and lowered her voice. "I have to go down to Key West for a meeting. Can you make sure the kids all get their dinner? Tracy should be home soon.''

''Wrong. She's staying in Key West tonight. She called a while ago.''

That gave her second thoughts. Maybe she shouldn't be taking off like this. Jason was old enough to baby-sit, but he didn't have a lot of experience at it and he didn't get along with the little ones the way Tracy did. With him in charge, she was likely to find all of the kids still up when she got home. A thought occurred to her.

''Have you heard from Hank tonight?'' she asked. ''Is he on his way to pick up Paul and Tommy?''

''I don't know.'' Jason's voice immediately turned surly as he sensed her lack of faith. ''Besides, we don't need him. I can watch the kids.''

She decided to risk it. Hank would have Paul and Tommy with him. Maybe it would be good for Jason to develop a sense of responsibility. Surely he could keep an eye on David and Melissa for a couple of hours. ''Okay. Make sure they get to bed on time.''

''Yeah.''

She'd hung up the phone and was halfway to the door when she began reconsidering. She flipped through her card file for the number that Hank had given her at the construction site in Marathon. After an instant's hesitation, she dialed. It rang and rang before finally being picked up by an answering machine. That reassured her. It must mean that he was already on his way home to pick up Paul and Tommy. Maybe when he found out she was out for the evening, he'd take the whole crew with him.

Relieved on all counts, including the fact that she was being saved from another close encounter with the man who'd been awakening her senses from a deep slumber, she closed the office door behind her and left for Key West.

When Hank walked into the kitchen after taking Paul and Tommy on a tour of the construction site, he found the counter littered with the makings of peanut-butter-and-jelly sandwiches. A trail of milk extended from the refrigerator to the kitchen table. Ann obviously wasn't home yet. He'd been hoping earlier that she'd be there in time to go along with him and the kids. He'd even considered waiting for her, but Paul and Tommy had been too eager to leave and he hadn't wanted to look quite so obvious about wanting to include Ann in the outing.

He was wiping off the counter when Jason came in.

"I was going to do that," he muttered defensively.

"It's no big deal. How about getting the milk off the floor before somebody slips?"

"You're so hot to clean up, do it yourself," Jason said, taking off and slamming the screen door behind him. Hank's temper kicked into overdrive.

"Jason, get back here this instant!" he ordered as he yanked open the back door and hit the porch at a run. Jason already had one foot in the yard, the other on the bottom step. He turned slowly and came back onto the porch.

"Who's gonna make me?" he said, facing Hank toe-to-toe, even though he stood barely shoulder height to him. Hank had to admire the kid's guts, if not his sense or his rotten attitude.

"You don't really need to ask that, do you? Now get back in here, mop up the milk and go to your room. While you're in there, do a little thinking about minding your manners. If I ever hear you talking to Ann the way you just sassed me, I'll tan your hide till they can use it for shoe leather."

"Real tough guy, huh? Why don't you just go back to Miami and leave us alone," Jason muttered, but he went back in and cleaned up the floor.

When Jason had stalked off to his room, Hank fixed himself a sandwich, took out a beer and sat down at the kitchen table to wait for Ann. He couldn't get his mind off Jason. The boy was trouble just begging to happen. Maybe what he needed, aside from some old-fashioned discipline, was an improved sense of self-worth. Maybe in the morning, after Jason had done a little thinking about his behavior, he'd talk to him about an after-school job. Good hard work and a little cash in his pockets might do wonders for him. He'd ask Ann about the idea tonight. If she agreed, he'd find something for him to do at the construction site.

Funny how he was starting to look forward to talking things over with her. He'd never been particularly anxious to get home after work before, but now he could barely wait to leave the office behind. It was nice having someone to share the day with, someone whose opinions he increasingly respected.

Face it, Riley, it's a hell of a lot more than that. She's getting under your skin.

All he'd been able to think about during the Super Bowl was the way her skin had burned beneath his touch, the way her cheeks had colored when he'd brushed them with his fingertips, the way her lips had parted breathlessly when he'd pressed an innocent good-night kiss against her brow. It had taken every ounce of willpower in him to keep from claiming more. He'd had to remind himself over and over that he had ruled out a casual affair with this woman days ago. His body, unfortunately, hadn't gotten the message. Even now it tightened at the vivid memories.

Where the hell was she? It was after eight and there was still no sign of her. He knew the nightly routine now. The little ones should have had their baths and been tucked in by eight. He walked into the living room and found Melissa still sitting in front of the TV, a thumb stuck in her mouth, her blanket clutched tightly in her other hand. Tommy, still wearing the hard hat Hank had given him, and Paul were racing their miniature cars around her. Despite the noise, it was obvious she could barely keep her eyes open. Someone had to take over in Ann's absence and it seemed he was elected. The unaccustomed role made him uneasy. He might be able to handle a hundred construction workers without blinking an eye, but these pint-size terrors still scared the daylights out of him.

"Okay, kids, bedtime," he announced in what he hoped was a convincing tone of voice. The boys scowled their protest, but Melissa just lifted her arms. He bent down and picked her up. Her arms circled his neck and her head rested under his chin. She smelled of baby shampoo and peanut butter. There was something about the combined scents that plunged him back more than thirty years. He wasn't crazy about that particular bit of time travel. He snapped himself back to the present, his voice rough. "Clean up the toys, Tommy, Paul. Then go get ready for bed."

"What about our baths?"

Hank groaned. How could he have forgotten the baths? Maybe they could get by without them for once. He looked at Melissa. She was as clean as she had been when Ann had helped her dress in the morning. He almost wished she were a little messier. It would have indicated that she'd played hard, instead of spending the day sitting quietly in front of the television afraid to get dirty, terrified of doing something wrong. The boys, however, were filthy from their streaked faces to their bare feet.

"You two guys go get cleaned up while I put Melissa to bed." He recalled their tendency to flood the bathroom. "And call me if you have any problems with the drain." As they started to race down the hall, he shouted one last warning. "And no water fights."

In Melissa's room, he struggled with the tiny, unfamiliar buttons on her blouse, then tugged off her shorts and searched for her pajamas.

"Where's Ann?" Melissa demanded sleepily.

"She'll be home soon," he promised. "She'll be in to give you a kiss as soon as she gets here."

"Want Ann," she protested, then stuck her thumb back in her mouth.

"I know you do, baby. She'll be here before you know it." He tried to get the pajama top on, but Melissa stubbornly refused to help. Her thumb left her mouth only long enough to ask plaintively again and again for Ann. Feeling utterly helpless, Hank awkwardly tucked her in and patted her head.

"Sleep tight, little one," he murmured, backing toward the door.

When he reached for the light switch, Melissa began to cry. "No go," she whimpered.

"I'm right here, baby," he said, turning off the light and plunging the room into darkness.

"No go!" Melissa wailed.

Responding instinctively to the genuine note of terror in her cries, he went back to the bed and sat down beside her. "Shh, little one. It's okay. I'm right here."

Melissa sniffed. As his eyes became accustomed to the dark, he saw that she was curled into a tight little ball, her whole body tense. All at once he recalled the lonely, scary nights he'd spent as a child, his mother away from home, some strange baby-sitter in the living room. The dark had been filled with all sorts of terrifying shadows. Ann would never let Melissa know that fear. He got up and searched the room, finally finding the tiny light plugged into a socket over the dresser. He switched it on.

"Is that better?" he murmured softly, looking down at the little girl whose body was finally relaxing. He reached out and rubbed away the last of the tears on the petal-soft cheeks. His throat tight with some overwhelming and unfamiliar emotion, he leaned down and touched a gentle kiss to that cheek. "Sweet dreams," he whispered.

Melissa wound her fingers trustingly around his thumb and sighed. Minutes later he heard the steady rise and fall of her breath. He tiptoed from the room, his heart filled to overflowing with sensations he couldn't identify, sensations that both frightened and intrigued him.

Tommy and Paul had finished their baths by the time he went to get them. The bathroom floor was under a sea of puddles. Plastic boats and toy animals were underfoot and soaked towels were scattered everywhere. For the most part, as near as he could tell, they had managed to wash off the worst of the dirt in the process of creating the watery havoc.

"Okay, guys, into bed."

"Will you come and tuck us in?"

Hugs and kisses later, the house was quiet. He knocked on David's door, poked his head in and found the boy doing his homework.

"Don't stay up too much longer."

"I won't."

"I wish you'd come with us tonight."

"It's okay. I had stuff to do here."

Hank nodded. "Maybe another time."

"Yeah, sure."

Sighing, Hank shut the door. David's aloofness saddened him, especially since he now knew the cause. He'd stayed behind tonight simply because he'd been afraid of doing something wrong. It was safer to stick with something familiar, to sit quietly in his room doing his homework. Nobody got angry at a straight-

A student. Nobody got rid of a thirteen-year-old who never made any noise. Hank vowed to keep trying to include him in more activities, to give him back his boyhood.

After Hank had cleaned up the bathroom, he went outside to wait for Ann. He took a beer with him and settled down in the hammock. Rocking it to and fro with one foot, he began drifting off. Rousing himself, he glanced at the illuminated dial of his watch. It was almost ten o'clock. He sat straight up, nearly tumbling from the hammock in the process.

"What the hell? Where is she?"

Ann would not go off and leave those children alone unless it had been an emergency. Now wait, he reminded himself. They hadn't been alone exactly. Jason had been there, which explained the makeshift dinner. Still, surely she should have been home by now. What if one of the kids had gotten sick? What if Melissa had had one of her dreams and had awakened frightened and crying? Jason couldn't have coped with that. The more he thought about it, the more furious he became.

It was typical female behavior. His own mother hadn't been able to stand the loneliness of the house at night. By the time he was ten he was used to the absences, accustomed to her flighty refusal to accept parental responsibility. His father had apparently had enough of her flirtations within the first year of the marriage. He had gone before Hank had even been born. The whole experience had colored Hank's relationships with women. He enjoyed them, appreciated their beauty the way a connoisseur appreciated a fine vintage wine, but he'd never wanted to possess one in any sort of lasting way. He'd learned from the cradle on that there was no such thing as a lasting commitment when it came to a woman.

Still, everything he'd discovered about Ann ran counter to that image. She'd always seemed rock solid, dependable. She was an instinctive nurturer, one of those people who gave a part of herself to everyone she met. She adored these kids. She'd never once given him any reason to doubt her love or her commitment to them. A blinding image of her car crashing made him sick to his stomach. He began pacing. If she didn't get home in the next half hour, he'd call the police. In the meantime, he'd ask Jason what he knew about her absence. Surely she'd at least called.

He tapped on Jason's door, then heard Paul's sleepy voice. He stuck his head in. Paul was blinking at him. There was no sign of Jason. Damn that kid. He'd obviously sneaked off the minute he heard Hank go outside.

The only thing left to do was wait. He paced some more. It was nearly midnight when he finally heard the car door slam and heard Ann's voice as she called out a cheerful good-night.

"Thanks, Tom. I'm glad I went."

Tom? He'd been tucking in kids and worrying himself sick and she'd been out on a date? He watched as she came around to the kitchen door.

"So you had a good time?" he said, his voice brimming over with sarcasm. He was furious with himself for believing that she was any different.

"Hank?"

"Who else were you expecting?"

"Is everything okay?"

"Everything is just swell. Next time you want a baby-sitter, though, I'd suggest you hire one."

Even in the dark, he could see her stiffen. Her arms folded around her waist. "What are you talking about?" she said defensively. "Jason was watching the kids."

"Wanna bet?"

"But I talked to him. He promised. Besides, I thought Paul and Tommy were going to be with you."

"They were. Once we got home, though, Jason took off without mentioning that you had a date."

"I did not have a date. I went to a meeting. I tried to call you, but you'd already left the office." A tense silence hung over them for several minutes before she finally took a deep breath and asked, "Is that the problem? You thought I had a date?" There was a note of surprise in her voice. He was too angry to acknowledge what it implied about her self-esteem.

"Why the hell should that be a problem?" he snapped. "You don't owe me anything."

"That's right, I don't. This household ran just fine before your arrival. I wasn't counting on you to look after the kids, so why are you in such a snit?"

"I am not in a snit."

"What would you call it?" she asked patiently.

Hank tried to analyze the emotions that were whirling through him. Relief at discovering that she was okay had quickly given way to anger and jealousy. "I was worried," he said finally. It was the only admission he had any intention of making. It was bad enough that she was so damn calm. He wouldn't have her laughing at him.

"I'm sorry. I thought Jason would explain. I went to Key West for a meeting about offshore drilling. It was unexpected or I would have told you about it this morning."

He nodded. He figured it was about as close to an apology as he was likely to get and probably about as much as he deserved after his sarcasm.

"How about a cup of tea?" she said quietly.

Despite himself, he grinned and felt himself beginning to relax. Tea. Ann's cure for everything. The world was clearly righting itself, getting back to normal.

"I'll sit with you while you have one. I'll have a beer."

He sat down in the kitchen and tilted his chair back on two legs, watching as she made the tea. There were no wasted motions, just quiet efficiency. Her expression, even after his irrational behavior, was unperturbed. That serenity conveyed itself to him, drawing him into the aura of warmth that seemed to surround her. He felt the last of the tension draining away.

"So tell me about Jason," she suggested, sitting down opposite him.

The muscles across the back of his shoulders knotted at once. "He's gone off somewhere," he said carefully, anticipating her panic.

"Gone off?" she said without the slightest evidence of concern. "What makes you think that?"

"I sent him to his room earlier. When I checked a while ago, he was gone."

She shrugged. "He's probably down by the water. That's where he goes whenever he's upset. He'll be back in an hour or so. What happened?"

"We had a fight over his attitude, as usual."

"Don't you think maybe you're a little hard on him? He is just a kid."

"I know and I had an idea. What would you think about my offering him a job? He could work after school, pick up a little money, maybe develop a better sense of responsibility."

Her eyes lit up. "You'd do that for him?"

"Why not?"

"I know you don't really trust him."

He didn't bother denying it. "Even so, maybe he just needs a break."

"That's exactly what he needs." She reached over and took his hand. "Thank you, Hank."

Startled by the impulsive gesture, Hank wasn't sure how to react. Ann kept him constantly off balance. With any other woman, the touch might have been an invitation. With Ann, it was nothing more than an innocent, friendly gesture of thanks. There was nothing at all innocent about his reaction, however. His pulse was hammering.

"Ann..." he began.

As if she'd guessed the change in his mood, the swift stirring of desire, she patted his hand affectionately once more, then withdrew.

"Tell me about your night," she suggested. Something in her penetrating gaze hinted that she was after more than a rundown on his experiences in getting the kids to bed. He doubted she gave a hang about what he'd watched on TV, either.

"It was quiet," he said, intentionally evading what he suspected she wanted to know. "Paul and Tommy had a great time at the construction site. I think Tommy's going to be a construction worker. It was all I could do to keep him from taking off across those girders. He's sleeping with the hard hat I gave him."

"I'm sure he loved all the attention."

"I couldn't talk David into going."

"I'm not surprised, but thanks for trying."

All the polite chitchat was beginning to grate on Hank's nerves, even though he was the one who'd started it. "This isn't really what's on your mind, is it?" he said finally.

"No."

"Go ahead. Say it."

"Your reaction when I got home, it was more than worry, Hank. You were really angry. Tell me why."

The fact that she sounded as much like a psychologist as a concerned woman really bugged him. He didn't want to be treated like one of her patients. He wasn't interested in baring his soul.

"You been reading those textbooks again, doctor?" he said.

She waited, her gaze intent.

He shrugged finally. Holding out was pointless. Ann was better at it than he was. She did it for a living. "Okay. Maybe I was jealous. Big deal."

She smiled. "I'm flattered, but I'm not convinced."

He tried to smile back. "I'm making a big admission here and you don't believe me? What's the deal?"

"Let's just say you're not a man whose confidence is easily shaken. Assuming for a moment that you were actually interested in me, you wouldn't be the least bit thrown by the fact that I'd spent the evening with another man. You'd chalk it up as a challenge."

Oddly enough, Hank realized that her analysis had a ring of truth to it. "Uncanny," he muttered under his breath.

She chuckled. "I'm a psychologist, Hank. Not a wizard."

"Same difference, if you ask me."

"You still haven't answered my question. What I really sensed underlying your anger was resentment. Is that possible?"

Hank thought back to all those unexplained absences that had tormented his childhood. "Maybe so," he admitted finally.

Ann's compassion reached out to him. He could feel it stealing over him, easing years of pain. "What happened?" she asked in that gentle tone that might have set off desire under other circumstances. Now, for some utterly absurd reason, it merely made him want to weep. He wasn't wild about the reaction. He hadn't shed a tear in more than twenty-five years, not since he'd finally figured out that things weren't ever likely to be any different.

"Hank?"

Despite his intention to curtail any private revelations, he found himself saying, "I guess I was just remembering some stuff I thought I'd put behind me."

"And you felt betrayed again," she guessed with more uncanny accuracy. Even without knowing the details, she'd struck on the truth.

He lifted his gaze to hers. A desire to be completely honest with her compelled him to admit it. "Maybe so. I got left behind all too often when I was a kid."

"I'm sorry."

"Hey, it was the kids you left on their own. Not me."

Ann shook her head. "They weren't alone, Hank. They had you."

"It's not the same."

"I think it's pretty darn good."

Her voice rang with quiet conviction, but he searched her face, looking for evidence of the easy comeback, the quick lie. He found sincerity. The last of his tension eased, replaced by a sudden need to hold her, to feel even closer to her. Then he was struck by a sudden and disconcerting revelation. He felt closer to Ann at this moment than he'd ever felt to any of the women he'd taken to his bed.

Could be he was growing up.

Could be he was heading for disaster.

Chapter Six

Something had changed between them. Ann noticed it at once the next morning. After reluctantly opening up to her, she had anticipated that Hank would be reserved. She had hoped for it, in fact. She desperately needed anything that would put a little distance between them. Instead, the expression in Hank's eyes was bolder than ever, more speculative. The atmosphere was as emotionally charged as if they'd made love. The edge of anticipation that teased her senses made her nervous.

Her wariness did not, however, keep her from snatching an entire box of jelly doughnuts from in front of Hank before he could swallow the first mouthful of sugar. She'd watched him devour about as many empty calories as she could without intervening. He watched the box go into the trash can with surprising equanimity. Heady with her success, she reached for his can of soda. He clamped it in a death grip.

"No way," he said. "I need this."

She decided it was only possible to wean an adult from so many bad habits at a time. She released the can.

"How about a nice bowl of oat bran?" she suggested cheerfully.

"I'd rather eat wood chips."

The grumpy remark brought forth giggles from the kids, who'd been avidly watching the contest of wills.

"Oatmeal, then?" she said, undaunted.

His injured gaze pierced her. "Is this some sort of punishment?"

"Take the oatmeal," David warned. "It's the best you're likely to get when she's on one of these health kicks. By the weekend she might loosen up enough to make pancakes."

"Not for you, you little traitor," she said, turning on David with mock ferocity and giving up the battle of wills with Hank. Let him figure out what to eat now that his doughnuts were in the garbage. "Where's Jason? Is he up?"

"I'm here," he said, skirting Hank's vicinity and dragging out the chair farthest from his nemesis. Ann could practically feel the animosity radiating from the teenager. She wondered if Hank could possibly bridge it or, for that matter, if he was even still planning to try.

"Morning, Jason," Hank said, practically willing the boy to look at him. Holding her breath, Ann waited.

Jason finally mumbled a greeting, but kept his eyes on his bowl of cereal. While the other kids chattered and began racing around to collect their books for school, Jason remained sullen and silent. The minute he'd finished, he scooted back from the table.

"Wait," Hank said.

"Gotta go."

"You have a few minutes. If you're late, I'll take you to school."

Jason shot a look at Ann that was clearly an appeal. "Sit down," she said gently. "Listen to what Hank has to say."

Grudgingly Jason sat back down, but his entire body was stiff. He clearly resented Hank and it was going to take an incredible effort to get through the barriers he'd erected.

"I got to thinking about something last night," Hank began. "A guy your age could probably use some extra cash, right?"

Ann saw the spark of interest that flared in Jason's eyes before he could hide it. Still, he gave a disinterested shrug.

"So I was wondering how you'd like to come to work for me after school and on Saturdays."

Jason's brief hint of interest vanished and with it Ann's hopes. Jason faced Hank with open hostility. "Work for you? No way I'm taking orders from you, man."

"Jason, that's no way to talk to Hank," Ann said. "Listen to him."

"Why should I? He's just trying to buy me off."

Hank, to his credit, ignored the bitter accusation. As if Jason had never spoken, he said, "You'll get a decent salary and you'll earn every penny of it. You'll be learning something new. Who knows, maybe you'll even like it enough that it'll help you decide on a career. That's something you should be starting to think about."

Jason ignored Hank and looked directly at Ann. "Do I have to?"

She glanced at Hank, who shook his head slightly. She sighed. "You don't have to, but I'd like you to think about it. A lot of kids your age would give anything for an opportunity like this. It's a chance to get some experience before you have to make a decision about college."

"Yeah," he said derisively. "I'm gonna go to Harvard on my looks, right?"

"Jason!" Hank warned.

Ann intervened. "You have good grades, Jason. Maybe we won't be able to afford an Ivy League school, but you can get a college degree if you want one badly enough. Working for Hank would be one way to begin getting some of the money you'd need. Think about this."

"That's all I'm really asking, son," Hank said. "Think about it. Talk it over with your buddies at school and see what they think. I'll bet a lot of them already have after-school jobs. You can give me your answer tonight."

His expression still sour, Jason gave a curt nod. "Okay. Now can I go?"

"Go," Ann said, exhausted by the exchange.

When he'd gone, she looked at Hank. "I see what you mean. His hostility's getting worse, instead of better. Maybe I've been blinding myself to it."

"You've just been loving him. And I've probably made it worse. Don't work yourself into a state over this. I can handle Jason," he said, drinking the last of his soda and getting to his feet.

"But you shouldn't have to. He's my responsibility."

Hank squeezed her shoulder reassuringly. "Uh-uh. He's old enough to take responsibility for himself. Have a good day, Annie."

After Hank had gone, with the warmth of his touch fading, but the memory of Jason's animosity still lingering, Ann wondered if a good day was even remotely possible. What if he was right about Jason? What if he was heading for trouble again? Was there anything she or even the two of them together could do to stop it?

That afternoon when the high school let out, Hank was waiting for Jason. He spotted him coming down the walk, books under his arm and a smile on his face. The slender, dark-haired girl beside him was laughing at something he'd said. When he spotted Hank, his expression sobered at once.

"What are you doing here?"

"I thought maybe we could finish our talk."

"I got nothing to say to you."

Hank permitted himself a slight grin. "Maybe not, but there are a few things I'd like to say to you."

"Save it for later. I'm busy."

"I'm sure your friend will forgive you," Hank said pointedly.

"It's okay, Jason," the girl said, smiling at Hank. "I gotta get home anyway."

Jason seemed about to argue, then his shoulders slumped. "I'll call you later."

"Great."

As soon as she'd gone, he whirled on Hank. "What'd you have to go and do that for? I don't need my friends thinking I've got some hard-ass truant officer breathing down my neck."

"I seriously doubt that's what she thought and even if it was, I'm sure you can set her straight. In the meantime, I want to talk to you about Ann."

To his surprise, Jason hesitated. "Is she okay? There's nothing wrong with her, is there?" There was genuine concern in the boy's voice. It gave Hank the first hope he'd felt in days.

"She's worried about you."

"That's only because you've gotten her all stirred up. We was getting along just fine until you came."

"You *were* getting along just fine."

"That's what I said."

Hank rolled his eyes. "Get in the truck. We can talk on the way."

"On the way where?"

"To your new job."

"I told you, man. I ain't working for you."

"Aren't, Jason. Do you ever crack that grammar book you've got under your arm?"

"I know enough to pass."

"And that's good enough for you? Just passing."

"It beats what my old man did. He dropped out when he was fifteen."

"And look how he wound up," Hank pointed out.

Jason looked as though he wanted to take a punch at him. Hank held up his hand. "Sorry. That was out of line. What I'm trying to say here is that you're too smart to waste your potential the way you've been doing. Ann went out on a limb for you. Don't you think you owe it to her to try a little harder?"

"She's never complained."

"Because she loves you. Maybe a little too much. She doesn't want to put extra pressure on you, but I think you're tough enough to take it. What do you think?"

"I'm tough enough to take anything you can dish out."

"Prove it. Start that job this afternoon. You won't be answering to me, if that's what you're worried about."

Jason clearly saw the trap that had been laid out for him. He also apparently realized there was no way around being snared, unless he wanted to show himself as a quitter. "I'll try it," he finally conceded. "But if I don't like it, I'm out of there."

"Fair enough."

Hank introduced him to the site foreman, then watched as Ted put him to work. By six o'clock Jason was dirty, hot and exhausted, but some of his belligerence had dimmed. Hank offered him a lift home.

"What the hell," Jason muttered, climbing into the pickup. "We're going to the same place."

At home, Jason walked through the kitchen like a kid asleep on his feet. Ann started to stop him, but Hank waved her off. "Let him go. He'll feel better after he's had a shower and some dinner."

"He took the job?"

"With a little prodding."

"Hank, you didn't back him into a corner, did you?"

"Maybe."

"But..."

"There's a door. He can always get out, if he wants to badly enough."

She nodded as Hank went off to take his own shower.

When he'd cleaned up and changed, he came back and found Ann sitting on the floor in the living room with Tommy and Melissa. Tommy, wearing his yellow hard hat, appeared to be in charge. They were building a skyscraper out of colored blocks. It was already tilting precariously.

Hank watched them for several minutes, enjoying the expression of fierce concentration on Melissa's face, the tolerant amusement on Ann's. "You'd better put something under the southwest corner," he advised Tommy finally.

"This is our development," Ann retorted. "You've got your own."

"Mine's bigger."

She shot a baleful look at him. "Bigger isn't necessarily better."

"Maybe not, but mine will still be standing in twenty years. Yours may not make it another twenty seconds." As if to prove his point, it wobbled under the weight of a red block Tommy was trying to add to the top. He knelt down and quickly inserted a block in the foundation. "There you go, partner. Steady as the Empire State Building."

"Is that tall?" Tommy wanted to know.

"Very tall."

"Want to see it," Melissa said.

"Maybe someday we can," he told her, his gaze locking with Ann's just as she tried to tell Melissa that it was too far away.

"Want to go," Melissa repeated.

"Someday," Hank repeated firmly, his eyes never leaving Ann's face, which was coloring under the direct gaze.

"What's for dinner?" he said at last, breaking the tension.

"Oh, my gosh," she said, jumping up and knocking over the tower in the process.

Melissa wailed. Tommy began gathering all the blocks and methodically going back to work. Hank dropped down to the floor. "I'll help, while Mommy gets dinner on the table."

"If I wasn't so terrified of what you'd fix, I'd send you to the kitchen," Ann said. "Nobody but an inveterate chauvinist would assume that cooking is woman's work, while building skyscrapers can only be done by big, tough men."

"Hey, I didn't say anything of the kind," he protested, laughing at her indignation. "I suspect that Melissa here could make a mighty fine engineer one day. I may even train her to follow in my footsteps."

Again he saw that off-guard look of wistfulness on Ann's face. His references to events far in the future seemed to rattle her even more than his touches. Perhaps she was right to be wary. How serious was he? The remarks seemed to come out without conscious thought on his part, indicating some subconscious direction in which he was heading without realizing it.

He blamed it on weeks of abstinence. Maybe he just needed to recall the experience of having a possessive woman back in his life again. A few carefully veiled references to commitment would put the fear of God back into him. Meantime, he was going to have to learn to think before he spoke.

Oddly enough, though, he couldn't keep his mind off the future all evening long. As he watched Ann, a yearning began to build inside him. He wondered what it would be like to know that this was the way it would be for the rest of his life, to know that she would always be there waiting for him, that he would be enveloped in that loving generosity of spirit that made her care for all these children as if they were her own.

He also wondered again why she was every bit as wary of the future as he was. What had scarred her so deeply? She'd learned many of his secrets, but what about hers?

While she put the kids to bed, he stretched out in the hammock, staring up at the inky sky. The scattering of stars seemed so much brighter here, away from the city lights. What did they hold for the future?

He heard the creak of the back door.

"Annie?"

"Yes."

"Come join me."

She took several steps in the direction of his voice, then hesitated as if she'd just realized where he was.

"Come on. There's room enough here for two."

"I don't think so. I really should go in and do the dishes."

"They'll wait. This sky won't. It may never be exactly this way again. One of those stars may fall."

"Why, Hank Riley, I do believe you may have the soul of a poet after all."

"I've always said you didn't give me enough credit for having a soul at all. Come on, Annie. How can you be afraid of a poet?"

He heard her low chuckle as she came closer. "They're the worst kind of romantic," she retorted.

He reached out, grabbed her wrist and pulled her into the hammock. She fell half-across him, torturing him with the press of her breasts against his chest, the whisper of her breath across his cheek. She struggled for just an instant, then seemed to sigh.

"Stay, Annie," he pleaded. "Right here beside me."

After a long hesitation during which he remained absolutely still, she lifted herself up from his chest and resettled herself beside him in the wide hammock. Her head rested on his shoulder.

"Watch for a shooting star," he said softly. "Then make a wish."

"Don't tell me you believe in all that?" she scoffed, her voice amused.

"You never know. I'm a firm believer in hedging all my bets."

"Are you a gambling man, Hank?"

It was an idle, teasing question, but he took it seriously. He thought about it for several minutes before saying honestly, "I never thought I was until recently."

"What's your game? Poker? Blackjack? Horses?"

"Love."

Ann's breath caught in her throat. "That's not a game."

"I've always played it as though it was. What about you? Have you ever been in love?"

"Once. A long time ago."

"What happened?"

She was quiet for so long he was afraid she might not answer, but it was a night made for sharing secrets. It was still enough and dark enough to hold a promise of endless privacy no matter what was revealed. "He left me."

There was a lifetime of raw pain behind those three simple words. "Why would any sane man ever leave a lovely woman like you?"

"Because," she said, her voice emotionless, "he was twenty-two and he was too young to want to be saddled with a wife and a baby."

Though there wasn't a sound besides the whisper of her voice and the occasional shriek of a gull, Hank knew she was crying. He could feel the dampness rolling from her cheeks onto his shirt, soaking it. The thought of her hurting for so many years made him ache inside. He wanted to enfold her in his embrace, to protect her from ever knowing such pain again, but he sensed that what she needed was to talk. He encouraged it by his silence.

"We were engaged," she began in a voice that was now roughened by tears. "But when I went to tell him about the baby, he got furious. He wanted to go to medical school. He had all these plans, you see. He blamed me for trying to ruin them. I tried to make him see that it would be okay, that we could manage, but he walked out. I never saw him again. The next day I lost the baby."

She laughed bitterly. "Ironic, isn't it? If he'd stuck around, we wouldn't have had anything to worry about."

"You would have been miserable with a selfish jerk like that."

"Maybe so, but at the time I thought my world had ended."

"And you've spent the rest of your life making sure that no other man could get close enough to inflict that sort of pain."

He felt her head shake.

"Yes, you have," he insisted. "Or you'd have found someone else by now. Instead, you've filled your life with all the children no one else wanted to make up for the one this man didn't want."

"Now who's playing psychologist?"

"Am I any good at it?"

"Not bad, actually."

"Ann..." he began, but she pressed a finger against his lips.

"Just because you know about my past doesn't change anything, though. Not between us."

"Are you so sure of that?" he said, kissing her gently. The taste of her tears was on her lips. He wanted to go on kissing her until the memory blurred and finally faded altogether. Instead, he held back and watched her.

"Are you sure?" he repeated.

Blue eyes, fringed by long, sooty lashes, gazed back at him expectantly and he lost track of what he'd meant to say to persuade her to let go of the past. Provocative images replaced all thoughts of idle conversation. He swallowed hard past the lump in his throat as he finally tore his gaze away.

"Maybe you ought to go get some sleep," he said finally.

She stared at him, then nodded. "Maybe so," she said softly.

For just an instant, Hank could have sworn he heard regret in her tone, but then she was on her feet and striding toward the house with that long-limbed gait that stirred him so.

It was nearly an hour later when he finally dared to follow her inside. He'd hoped she'd gone to bed, but he found her at the sink, rinsing off dinner dishes with those familiar, sure movements. She'd changed clothes. A man's wool plaid shirt hung nearly to her knees. Her legs were bare down to the bright yellow socks that had settled in folds at her ankles.

Looking at those legs was dangerous, he decided at once. Taking a beer from the refrigerator, his eyes locked instead on the movement of her hands, soft and slippery against the fragile porcelain. He imagined them sliding over his flesh with the same gentle touch, the same deft strokes, water cascading around them, cooling their burning flesh. His blood surged at the image. He could hear the pounding of his heart, feel the throbbing low in his abdomen. His grip on the bottle of beer was so tight, he was afraid the glass would snap. If she didn't get out of the kitchen in the next five minutes, he was going to forget all of his honorable intentions and take her right there.

As if she'd guessed his thoughts, she turned suddenly. His expression must have confirmed what she'd sensed, because the cup fell from her hands and shattered on the tile floor. Her lips parted on a gasp of dismay and her eyes widened at the noise, but she didn't look away from him for even a fraction of a second. It was as if she were waiting for him to act, daring him to, wanting him to.

"I thought you'd gone to bed," she said shakily.

Silent, Hank moved slowly toward her, watching the flare of excitement in her eyes.

"Do you know what you're doing to me, Annie?" he murmured as his fingers caressed the curve of her jaw, then tangled in her hair. She nodded. "I want you, Annie love. Now. Tonight."

Again she nodded and Hank felt the tension inside him shatter like the teacup. He leaned down and touched his lips to hers again, his fingers light against the pulse in her neck. It jerked convulsively, then ran wild. His own senses took off at a matching gait as his tongue invaded the sweet recesses of her mouth. He gave himself up to the kiss, exploring, tasting. Her soft cries of pleasure broke over him with the force of magnificent ocean waves.

"We'll be good together, Annie. I promise you that."

"I know," she whispered against the burning column of his neck, her fingers now wound tightly in his hair.

The swell of her breasts was evident beneath that oversize shirt. At the stroking of his fingertips, the peak hardened at once. He bent to capture it in his mouth, his hand moving on, drifting lower over her flat stomach, then finding the warm mound between her thighs. She gasped as he rubbed the flat of his palm rhythmically back and forth. Her hips arched into the strokes.

He lifted his head and watched her. Her head was thrown back, leaving her neck vulnerable to his kisses. Her lips were parted as her breathing came in increasingly rapid bursts. He lifted the hem of the shirt and ran his fingers up the inside of her thigh. Her eyes widened as his hand once again touched the heat between her legs, this time with only the most delicate silk as a barrier. He could feel her moistness and it almost drove him wild. If this kept up, he would take her here and now. The heat exploding through him demanded he do just that.

Some guardian angel with a perverse sense of timing stopped him. Or perhaps it was the fleeting look of panic that he'd caught in her eyes before she'd determinedly banished it and given herself up to his loving.

He removed his hand and allowed the shirt to glide back down. It didn't cover nearly enough of those long, slender legs.

"Hank?" she said, her expression puzzled.

He sighed heavily with regret.

"It's okay, Annie love." He pressed a chaste kiss to her forehead. "It's okay."

"But I wanted you to make love to me."

"I know you did and God knows I wanted to."

"Then why are you stopping?"

"Because it would be wrong. I can make you want me in your bed, but that's not good enough for you. After what you've been through, you're the kind of lady who deserves forever. I don't believe in it."

"I'm all grown-up, Hank. I can make my own decisions. I have no illusions anymore. There were no demands connected to this, no expectations."

He smiled. "You may not think so now, Annie, but I guarantee you in the morning, you'd have felt differently. Neither one of us would have been able to live with the guilt." He touched her swollen lips with the tips of his fingers and tried to ignore the hurt in her eyes. "Now go to bed, before I change my mind."

She turned back to the sink, her shoulders tensed.

He reached out and touched her. She shuddered visibly, which made him feel like crying.

"Go, dammit," he said, his voice gruff. "I'll finish the dishes."

"It's my house," she reminded him, with an all-too-familiar mixture of stiff-necked pride and indignation.

"Meaning?" Hank said.

A plate clattered to the floor, shattering. Ann clung to the edge of the counter so tightly, he could see the whitening of her knuckles. He bent down to pick up the shards of china as he waited for her to answer.

"Meaning you don't give the orders. If anybody goes anywhere tonight," she said in a tight, controlled voice, "it ought to be you."

Grateful for the anger that was escalating by the second, he whirled her around, ready to lash out.

She lifted her chin and stared back. Defiant. Proud. Furious.

Want thundered through him. He held it at bay by sheer will.

"Fine," he said when he could control his voice. "If that's the way you want it, I'm out of here."

Chapter Seven

It was practically the middle of the night and he was beat, but Hank couldn't get away from Ann's fast enough. Gravel flew. Dust curled up behind the pickup as he bounced over the rutted driveway and sped onto U.S. 1 heading north toward home.

Toward sanity.

And, face it, toward safety.

The last bounce, which very nearly sent his head through the roof, reminded him that he'd been meaning to fill in the potholes before Ann's car broke its axle. The fact that he was still thinking of the chores that needed to be done around her house infuriated him all over again. She was independent. She didn't need or want him around. She'd made that plain enough when she'd kicked him out just now. She sure as hell didn't need him making love to her, either. Why couldn't she see that?

And why the hell couldn't he leave well enough alone? Why had he gone and practically seduced the woman over the kitchen sink when he knew just how wrong it would be for both of them? He was no over-sexed kid who didn't know how to keep his pants on. He'd never in his life allowed things to go so far with a woman who wasn't fully aware of the score. Like he'd told Ann, not only didn't she know the score, she didn't even know the name of the game.

He turned the radio on full blast, hoping to drown out his thoughts. Unfortunately he was tuned to a country station. He'd forgotten that the lyrics of half the songs out of Nashville were all too explicit about the pitfalls of loving the wrong woman. He should have switched the dial. Somehow, though, he felt he deserved the torment. By the time he'd gotten halfway back to Miami, he was thinking very seriously of just walking away, of turning the whole damn Marathon job over to Todd.

Or murdering him for sending him down there in the first place. As for Liz, he might never forgive her for suggesting this living arrangement.

He was not, therefore, in a particularly welcoming frame of mind at ten in the morning when Todd turned up on his doorstep while he was still tossing and turning and trying to get the first minute's sleep of the endless night. Yanking open the door at what seemed like dawn to find his cheerful, wide-awake partner on his doorstep set his teeth on edge. He scowled, then stomped back inside. Leaving Todd to make what he would of the irritable behavior, he climbed into the shower, turned it to its iciest temperature and stood under it for fifteen minutes. It didn't do a damn thing except make him shiver.

Tugging on a pair of well-worn jeans and an old shirt that he didn't bother to button, he went into the kitchen. He didn't even growl a thank-you for the mug of coffee Todd handed him in silence. He took a couple of swallows of the strong brew, sat the cup on the counter and began slamming pots and pans into the kitchen cupboard. Undaunted, Todd failed to heed the cues to leave.

"How's it going?" Todd asked instead, leaning nonchalantly against the doorjamb watching Hank's performance.

Deliberately misinterpreting the how's-life-in-general scope of the question, Hank said, "We're on schedule."

"No problems?"

"Not since you got that supplier straightened out."

"How's Ann?"

The question sounded innocent. Hank's reaction was not. His gut knotted the way an alcoholic's would at a casual reference to fourteen-year-old Scotch—with longing. He managed a disinterested shrug. It was the greatest acting of his life. "Fine, I suppose."

"You suppose? You see the woman every day. Don't you know for sure?"

"She's a hard woman to read."

"Oh, really? I've always thought of Ann as being the most straightforward, honest woman around. No subterfuge. No games."

"We don't sit around having conversations about her state of mind or her health," he snapped, then gave another offhand shrug. "Like I said, she seems about the same as when I arrived, so I guess that means she's fine."

Todd, damn him, laughed. "She's getting to you, isn't she?"

"Right," he retorted sarcastically. "Like poison ivy."

"Hmm."

He shot a glance at the man he'd known for most of his life. Todd was looking very smug. "Don't stand there gloating, old buddy, or you'll be down in Marathon before you can say goodbye to your wife and children. In fact, with the mood I'm in, I don't care if that sweet, innocent baby of yours doesn't see you again before she turns eighteen."

"That bad, huh?"

Despite the early hour, Hank grabbed a beer from the refrigerator, took a long, slow swallow, then sighed wearily. Further denials were pointless. Todd had always been able to guess what was going on in his head anyway. They'd bolstered each other up during crises far more devastating than this one.

"Worse," he admitted. "But hardly cataclysmic."

"Want to talk about it?"

"There's nothing to say."

"You falling for her?"

"Hell, no."

"Oh, really?"

Todd sounded incredibly skeptical. Hank resumed glowering and slamming things around. "Don't push it," he muttered.

"I don't get it. What's wrong? Ann's intelligent, attractive. You're both single. I've never known you to miss out on an opportunity to expand your dating circle."

"Ann Davies is not my type," he insisted.

"She's a woman."

"Very funny."

"Come on, give. What's not to like?"

"She's a terrific lady, okay? Is that what you wanted to hear? That doesn't mean we get along."

"I think I'm beginning to get the picture. Is she, by any chance, trying to reform you?"

"She took away my damn doughnuts," he retorted before he could stop himself.

A sound suspiciously like the beginning of a hoot of laughter was quickly smothered. "That's serious all right."

"She wants me to eat oat bran," he added indignantly. "Can you believe it? The woman does nothing but preach about cholesterol from morning to night. If I eat any more fresh vegetables, I'll grow ears like Peter Rabbit. I haven't had a decent steak in the past two weeks. Every time I sneak a cheeseburger for lunch I feel like I ought to go straight to a priest and confess."

"Just tell her how you feel. She's a reasonable woman."

Hank stared at Todd incredulously. "Are we talking about the same woman? The woman who threatened to pour all of my sodas down the drain? The woman who gets hysterical at the sight of potato chips?''

''Don't you think you're exaggerating just a little?''

''Exaggerating? If anything, I'm downplaying the way that woman is trying to run my life.''

''I'm sure she's just thinking of your health.''

''Maybe I should bring her a note from my doctor.''

''If your doctor knew what you ate, he'd probably swear out a warrant and lock you up in a hospital for a month to wean you off all of that junk.''

''You sound just like Ann.''

''Well, she does have a point. You're at that age.''

''What age? I'm thirty-seven. I exercise. I haven't had any complaints from the women I date about my stamina.''

''Do you have a date for tonight?''

''What does that have to do with anything?''

''Do you?''

''No.''

Exaggerated astonishment registered on Todd's face. ''Hank Riley is back in town and doesn't have a date! Women across Dade County must be in the throes of despair.''

Hank's eyes narrowed. Todd chuckled. ''Why are you here, by the way? I tried to reach you in the Keys and Ted said you hadn't come in or called. Ann didn't make a lot more sense when I called there.''

''You talked to Ann?'' he said, suddenly wary.

''How else do you think I knew you were here?''

''How'd she sound?''

"Like Ann. Dammit, Hank, what the devil is going on between you two?"

"Nothing."

"If you hurt her, Liz will kill you. Come to think of it, I may kill you. She's been a good friend to us. Kevin, needless to say, adores her. She's turned his life around since she's been helping him with his reading problem."

"Who the hell says I hurt her? Did she say that?"

"*She* didn't say anything. Ann is the soul of discretion, in case you haven't noticed. I'm picking up all these weird vibes from you."

"Well, you've got it all wrong."

"Okay, we'll forget that for the moment and go back to the other issue you seem to be evading. What brings you to Miami?"

Good question. Hank knew he should have anticipated it, but he hadn't. He'd been too busy running for his life. "I, um, I had some things to follow up on in the office."

"What things?"

"Things, okay?"

"Interesting."

"Don't get cute with me, buddy. I'm too damn tired to deal with your smart remarks."

The admission cost him. It said far too much about the sleepless nights he'd spent in the past couple of weeks, as well as his current state of mind. He caught the twitch of Todd's lips. It rankled.

"Have dinner with Liz and me," Todd suggested.

Hank visibly recoiled from the daunting prospect. "Oh, no. Not a chance."

"How come? Don't you want to see your godson? He could use a few pointers on his pitching. And the baby is almost crawling. You should see her."

"I have spent the past two weeks surrounded by rug rats. I do not need to see any more. Cute as yours might be," he amended, knowing exactly how touchy Todd could be over his offspring.

"We'll fix steaks on the grill."

His mouth began to water.

"And I just bought a case of cabernet sauvignon that will go perfectly with them."

He weakened. Obviously in the past couple of weeks his resistance had been shot to hell along with his nerves. It was pathetic. "What time?"

"Eight."

"Make it seven. I doubt if I'll be able to stay awake past nine and I'd hate to fall asleep before I get the first bite of steak."

"Great. See you later, pal. What time are you coming in to the office?"

"The office?" he repeated blankly.

"You did say that's why you came, didn't you?"

"Oh, right. Later."

"Later," Todd repeated, clearly amused. "Good time."

As soon as his still-smirking partner had left, Hank's thoughts whirled right back to Ann. He recalled a dozen different images, all of them tantalizing enough to set his blood on fire.

"No way," he muttered as he began to scrub the kitchen floor. It was a task he usually left to the maid. She came once a week. The floor was spotless. He didn't care. Scrubbing it kept him from pounding on walls. As he mopped, he forced himself to itemize every one of Ann's innumerable flaws aloud.

"Bossy." An image of her comforting Melissa countered it.

"Opinionated." He recalled how intently she'd listened to Tracy's problems at school, never once offering advice, only encouragement. Tracy had worked out her own solution and left for Key West with renewed confidence.

"She has no sense of style." She'd been wearing a man's wrinkled red plaid flannel shirt when he left and bright yellow socks. That shirt had barely reached to midthigh. To his astonishment, it had triggered sensations more powerful than the most seductive black lace teddy. Judging from the renewed racing of his pulse, its power hadn't dimmed over the past few hours. He tried harder to counteract the effect.

"That impossible hair!" A memory of his callused fingers tangled in the short, dark strands made his muscles go taut.

"Oh, hell!"

Ann was scrubbing pots and pans with a vengeance. She had already mopped the kitchen floor, vacuumed the house from one end to the other and dusted so thoroughly that the kids had scattered. She was considering washing all the windows next. It probably wouldn't help.

Hank Riley was the most infuriating, insensitive, nervy man she'd ever met. Last night had been...a disaster. An unmitigated disaster. What had ever made her think that she wanted that man in her bed? What had possessed her to even allow him into her house? In only a few weeks he'd done more to turn her well-ordered life upside down than any four of the children combined. Once he had gone for good, she was sure she'd feel quite capable of coping with another half-dozen kids.

"Ann?"

She turned and saw Tracy regarding her hesitantly. "What's up, kiddo? I thought you'd spent the night down in Key West."

"I did. I just thought I'd come back this morning."

"No classes?"

"It won't hurt me to skip 'em for once."

"No. Probably not," Ann said, studying her more closely. She sounded very defensive and she seemed a little pale. "Are you sure you're okay?"

"I said I'm fine," Tracy snapped, then flushed guiltily. "Sorry. Where's Hank?"

"I'm not sure. I assume he's at work."

"He's not. I checked there."

"Why?"

"I just wanted to ask him something."

"Can't you ask me?"

Tracy shook her head and Ann felt somehow betrayed.

"You sure?"

"Yeah. It's about guys."

"I see." She considered pressing, but decided against it. With her track record in the past twenty-four hours, she was the last person to be giving out advice about men. "Maybe he went up to Miami. You could call the office there. If he's not in, I'm sure someone there will know how to find him."

Tracy's expression brightened at once. "You have the number?"

"It's on the pad by the phone under Todd's name."

Tracy flung her arms around her. "Thanks, Ann."

Ann watched as she copied the number and raced to use the phone in the living room. Again that stirring of resentment nagged at her.

"This is just terrific, Ann, old girl. Now you're jealous of the man."

It was true. She'd noticed it more than once as Hank began slowly interacting with each of the children. Despite his reservations, he was really trying to reach Jason. As for Tommy and Paul, they clearly idolized him. It had hurt her the first time she'd realized how often they turned to Hank. They trailed him around the house, imitating his mannerisms. Tommy constantly wore the tiny hard hat Hank had gotten him. Now Tracy was defecting as well.

Ann shook her head and sighed. She ought to be grateful. She analyzed the emotions that were rampaging through her. Gratitude wasn't among them. Nope. Jealousy was at the top of the list.

"Well, you'll just have to get over this in a big hurry," she muttered, pouring vinegar and water into a bucket and heading for the windows that faced the Atlantic.

Filled with trepidation, Hank approached Todd's house in Coconut Grove later that night. He knew that his encounter with Todd in the morning had been little more than polite chitchat compared to the cross-examination Liz was likely to subject him to. He wasn't sure he was up to it.

Ever since Tracy's phone call, he'd been tempted to head straight back down to the Keys. He didn't like the sound of this boy she was going out with. He guessed the kid's hormones were in overdrive and he wasn't one bit sure that all his advice had equipped Tracy to deal with him. His stomach knotted at the thought of the jerk laying a hand on that sweet, innocent kid. After the hell her old man had put her through, she deserved never again to be touched except with love and respect.

He wasn't aware that he'd been sitting in the car for some time until he heard Kevin shouting at him.

"Hey, Hank, come on! Dad said you'd help me with my pitching. It's only a little while till dinner."

Hank mustered a grin, grabbed the baseball mitt he'd thrown in the back and climbed wearily from his truck. At least it would provide a reprieve from Liz's inquisition.

"Okay, kid, let's see what you've got."

Todd came out moments later and joined them on the wide sweep of lawn. "Sorry I missed you at the office. Feeling any better?"

"I'm great."

"Right."

Hank shot him a vicious look, then turned pointedly to Kevin. "Try a curveball. You remember where I told you to put your fingers."

The ball zipped toward him with surprising speed and accuracy, landing in his mitt with a solid thud. Kevin's grin split his freckled face. "How's that?"

"Not bad, kid. You've been practicing."

"Every night. At least when Dad gets home in time. Liz tried to catch for me one night, but she was pretty bad," he confided. His tone and his face registered his disgust. "Girls!"

Hank laughed. "Yeah, kid, I know just what you mean."

"I heard that," Liz called, poking her head out the front door. "People who make unkind remarks about .he cook get steaks that are the consistency of shoe .eather."

Hank immediately adopted a suitably contrite expression and jogged over to plant a kiss on Liz's orehead. "Sorry. Present company excepted, of course."

"Thank you." She glanced toward Kevin. "And you?"

Kevin grinned at his stepmother. "Sorry, Liz."

She nodded in satisfaction. "Good. Then dinner's ready."

Hank made the first cut into his thick, juicy steak with the enthusiasm of a half-starved man. He lifted the bite to his mouth, savored the aroma, then bit into it slowly. It was delicious, with just a hint of mesquite in the flavor. He swallowed and the image of Ann's disapproving expression flickered alive in his stupid brain. Guilt stole in. The second bite wasn't nearly as flavorful as the first. The third practically choked him.

He determinedly ate another and then another, forcing himself to finish the entire steak.

When he looked up from his meal at last, he caught Todd and Liz exchanging an amused glance.

"Did you enjoy your steak?" Todd inquired with contrived innocence.

"Terrific."

"I have another piece in the kitchen," Liz offered sweetly.

"No, thanks. I've had plenty."

"More salad?" She held out the bowl.

Hank reached for it, then stubbornly jerked back his hand. "No."

"Are you sure? You've hardly eaten a thing."

He took a deliberate sip of the excellent full-bodied wine. "Guess I just wasn't as hungry as I thought."

"Aren't you feeling well?" Liz persisted, her eyes filled with concern.

"I'm fine. Dinner was superb."

"How about some apple pie?"

Hank was cheered by the prospect. Apples were healthy. Not even Ann could find anything to object to there.

"Maybe with some vanilla ice cream on top?" Liz suggested.

His mouth watered. "Terrif—" he began, then recalled Ann's speech about the fat content of ice cream as she'd given him a bowl of frozen yogurt. "No. I'll take it plain."

Damn. She wasn't within fifty miles and she was still ruining his appetite. Fortunately before Liz could make too much out of his refusal, the phone rang.

"I'll get it," she said. "Kevin, how about bringing the dishes into the kitchen."

When the two of them had gone, Todd said quietly, "It's worse than you've admitted, isn't it?"

"Don't you dare start gloating again."

"I wouldn't dream of it. I've waited a long time to witness the fall of the mighty lecher. Are you in love with her?"

"Absolutely not. You know how I feel about love. It doesn't exist."

"Methinks thou does protest too much."

Hank glared. "Think whatever you want."

"Well, what are you going to do about it?"

"Not a damn thing," he insisted stubbornly.

"But . . ."

Liz's voice interrupted Todd's protest. "Hank, the call's for you. It's Tracy."

He knocked over his chair in his haste to get to the phone. Ignoring Liz's half-amused expression, he grabbed for the phone. "Are you okay?" he asked, his voice raw with panic.

All he heard were muffled sobs.

"Tracy, where are you?"

"At a gas station."

"Where?"

"In Key Largo."

"Are you okay?" He closed his eyes and forced himself to ask gently, "He didn't hurt you, did he?"

"No, I'm just so mad." She choked back another sob. "Hank, he was just as big a creep as you said he was. Why didn't I listen to you?"

Hank's heart finally began beating again. "Because you wanted to believe in the guy. Trusting someone isn't a sin. It takes a lot of experience, though, before you can completely trust your judgment."

"I'm never dating again."

Hank grinned, thankful that Tracy couldn't see it. "I doubt you'll feel that way by next weekend. You stay put, honey. I'll come get you."

"You don't have to do that," she said bravely, but her voice was still thick with tears. "I can call Ann."

"Stay put. I'm on my way." He took down the location of the gas station and hung up, then turned to find Liz regarding him intently.

"You heard?"

She nodded.

"I have to go get her."

Liz reached out and touched his arm. Until he felt the gentle brush of her fingers, he hadn't realized how tense he was. "She'll be fine. She's just scared."

He felt himself beginning to relax. "I know."

He headed for the door, then turned back. "Thanks."

"Any time." Before he could close the door, she called out. "Hank."

He looked back.

"You'll make a wonderful father."

He shook his head, but as he climbed back into his truck and headed south, he realized that was exactly how he felt: like a father.

It scared the hell out of him.

Chapter Eight

Tracy was waiting exactly where Hank had told her to wait, inside the office at the gas station. Sitting on a chair, shoulders slumped, her expression glum, she looked like an abandoned waif, rather than a beautiful young woman just emerging into adulthood. Seeing her like that scared him. He didn't have any experience at handling something like this. What if he said the wrong thing? What if he only made matters worse? How had Todd survived all the years he'd been a single parent to Kevin? How did Ann cope on her own with the steady stream of kids she'd taken into her home and heart? He wished he'd taken the time to call her for some quick advice on parenting before barreling down here, but he hadn't. He was on his own.

He opened the door to the office and stepped inside.

"Tracy," he said quietly.

Her gaze shot up and her eyes filled with tears. She launched herself into his arms and clung like a frightened child. He held her tight. "It's okay, sweetheart. Everything's okay," he soothed.

He turned to the attendant. "Thanks for letting her stay inside."

"No problem, mister. I just wish more girls used their heads these days and called home when things got out of hand."

When they'd gotten into the car, Hank handed her a tissue. "He's right, you know. You did the right thing by calling. Don't ever be afraid to turn to Ann or me when you're in trouble."

Tracy fidgeted nervously. She glanced sideways at him.

"What's wrong?" he asked.

"You're not going to tell Ann, are you?"

He hesitated, torn. Finally he sighed. "Not unless you say it's okay."

"Thank you."

"Wait a minute. I think you should talk to her about it yourself."

"But she wouldn't understand."

It was the cry of teenagers about their parents from time immemorial, but still Hank stared at her in astonishment. "Ann? Sweetheart, she's the most understanding woman around. Of course she'd understand."

"But she's so perfect. She never makes any mistakes, at least not really dumb ones like this."

Hank thought of the story Ann had told him just last night about her own youthful error in judgment. If only she would share that story with Tracy. It would bring the two of them even closer, bridging the gap that even Ann was all too aware of.

"Talk to her," he urged again. "I think you could be surprised."

An hour later when they walked into the house together, Ann looked up from her book, her expression welcoming until she spotted Hank with Tracy. Alarm warred with dismay. Hank could read the entire gamut of emotions in her eyes. As always, concern for one of her kids won out over her own feelings.

"Is everything okay?" she asked, looking anxiously from one to the other.

"Fine," Tracy mumbled, not meeting her gaze directly. "I'm going to sleep. Thanks for picking me up, Hank."

When she'd gone, Ann stared hard at Hank. "Is she really okay?"

He nodded. "Just a little shaken."

"What happened? Was there an accident? Why was she with you?"

"I gave her a ride home."

"Don't be deliberately obtuse. Why?"

"Ask her."

"Dammit, Hank. She's practically my daughter. If she's in some kind of trouble, I ought to know about it."

He knelt down beside her so he could gaze directly into her worried eyes. He placed a reassuring hand on her knee, but removed it when he felt her go tense.

"She's okay, Annie. I swear it, but I promised her I wouldn't talk about it. I think she'll tell you herself once she's had some time to settle down a bit."

She frowned at him, then asked furiously, "Where the hell do you get off deciding what's best for one of my kids? I'm responsible. Whatever happened, I should have been there, not you."

He recognized the frustration and guilt in her voice and wanted more than anything to put her fears to rest, but he'd made a promise and he intended to keep it. He knew enough about teenagers to understand that Tracy would never trust him again if he betrayed her now, no matter how well-intentioned he might be.

"She called me," he reminded her gently. "What was I supposed to do?"

After a long silence, she finally let out a deep breath. "I'm sorry. You're right. You had to go. I shouldn't have taken it out on you, but, Hank, I'm really worried about her. She was acting funny all day long."

"She really is fine."

"I'm not so sure. I'm not just talking about whatever happened tonight. I'm talking about how she handled it. She insisted on calling you earlier today, too. I'm sure that was part of the same thing. I think she's developing a full-scale crush on you."

The comment hit him from out of the blue. It rocked him back on his heels. "Come on, Annie. Don't be ridiculous."

"It's not ridiculous and you know it. You may well be the first man who's ever treated her with respect and tenderness. Why wouldn't she fall for it?"

"Hell, I'm old enough to be her father."

"Age is irrelevant in a situation like this. Young women who've had absent or abusive fathers often think they're in love with older men who are like the idealized fathers they never had."

He got up and started pacing. The movement only seemed to increase his agitation. Finally he sank down in a chair and ran his fingers through his hair. Ann was making a sort of twisted kind of sense, but he was convinced she was way off base. He wasn't that insensitive. He would have known if Tracy had a crush on him.

"You're wrong, Annie. She's thinking of me as her father. I'm sure that's all it is."

"Maybe. Just be careful. Whatever her feelings, if she begins to depend on you too much, she's going to be devastated when you leave."

"Who says I'm leaving?"

"Hank, be realistic," she said impatiently. "The job will be over sooner or later. You'll go back to Miami. We may all run into one another occasionally on holidays at Liz and Todd's but that will be the extent of it."

He studied her closely. Her expression was determinedly unemotional, her tone flat. Still, he had a feeling she was voicing her own fears now. "Is it Tracy you're worried about now or yourself?"

She flushed. "Leave me out of this. I'm an adult. I can handle it."

"Can you really? Look what happened last night."

"Nothing happened," she pointed out with a touch of wry humor.

"I was referring to how upset you got, but let's put that aside for a minute and deal with what's really bothering you. You know perfectly well that I stopped making love to you for all the reasons you're talking about. I probably will go back to Miami in a few months and when I go, I don't want you on my conscience."

"How very noble!" she said, her blue eyes flashing fire. "Don't do me any favors, mister."

Troubled by the hurt behind her remark, Hank tried to sort through the mess they seemed to be in. "Do you want me to move out now? Maybe it would be better for everyone if I went before the attachments got any deeper." That went for him as well as them, though he wasn't willing to admit it.

"Maybe it would be," Ann said in a voice that was surprisingly weak considering her angry state only moments earlier.

There was a sharp ache in his gut, but Hank nodded and got to his feet. "I'll pack my things."

He was halfway across the room when he heard what sounded like a muffled sob. When he turned, Ann was hastily wiping the tears from her cheeks. He was beside her in an instant. Kneeling again, he took her hands in his. "Annie, is this really what you want?"

The broken sound she uttered was part laugh, part sob. "I don't seem to know what I want," she confessed. "For the first time in a very long time I don't have the vaguest idea what's right."

"Then I guess we're in the same boat. I don't seem to be sure of anything anymore, either. Liz and Todd seem to have this crazy idea we're meant for each other. They set us up, you know.''

She nodded and smiled ruefully. ''Think we should wring their necks?''

''It's crossed my mind. On the other hand, they are our best friends. They know us pretty well.''

''What are you saying?''

''Maybe we should stay right where we are and play out this hand like a couple of grown-ups.''

''Now that's a risky notion,'' she joked feebly. Tears trembled on the ends of her lashes, then spilled down her cheeks.

''Hey, I'm a gambling man, remember?''

''Maybe so, but *I've* never gambled on anything in my life.''

With the pad of his thumb, he rubbed away her tears. ''Who knows,'' he said. ''Maybe you'll have beginner's luck.''

The only trouble with this new game plan was that they didn't seem to know how to begin. For the next few days, they were both so wary Ann thought she would scream in frustration. Every time Hank so much as brushed accidentally against her, he apologized profusely and bolted. She was rapidly reaching the end of her patience.

Nor was she one bit sure how she felt about Hank's decision to insinuate himself into their lives more completely than ever. From her point of view, particularly after their talk about Tracy, she still thought a little caution was called for. When she told him exactly that one night after dinner, he snapped back,

"You can't have it both ways. I can't stay here and back off at the same time."

"I don't see why not," she said stubbornly.

He simply stared at her.

"Okay, so it's not logical," she admitted finally. "I'm not feeling very rational."

"How are you feeling?"

"Like I'm being ripped in two."

"Me, too."

Suddenly she started laughing. The whole thing was utterly absurd. They were two supposedly mature, rational adults with advanced college degrees. Between them, surely they had sufficient brainpower to come up with a solution.

"I'm not sure I see what's so funny," Hank growled. "We've got a problem here."

"Exactly. Would you care to define it?"

"We're . . ." He fumbled for an explanation.

"Horny," she provided.

"Annie!" Shock registered on his face, though she could see from the look in his eyes that she'd hit the nail on the head. Hank was not a man used to going for long without a woman in his life. Ironically, he was probably equally adept at avoiding emotional intimacy. In their current situation, the tables had been turned on him.

"Well, that's the problem, isn't it? If I were any other woman, you'd have taken me to bed days ago, wouldn't you?"

"You are not any other woman."

"I suppose I should thank you for that," she said dryly. "But at the moment I'm not one bit grateful."

He chuckled. "I see your point."

They sat there staring at each other. "We could go to a movie," he suggested finally.

"It is nearly ten o'clock at night."

"We could rent one."

"And sit side by side, curled up on the sofa," she said, deliberately taunting him.

"Bad idea."

"I knew you'd see it."

"How about chess? We could play a game of chess. It's dull, hardly the stuff of erotic fantasies."

"I don't play chess."

"Checkers, then. Hell, help me out here, Annie. I'm trying."

"Okay, checkers. I think Paul has a set in his room."

"You get 'em. I'll make a bowl of popcorn."

"I should have known you'd try to sneak in junk food."

"I'll bring grapes for you."

Fifteen minutes later they had the checkerboard on the table between them, along with a bowl of buttered popcorn and a plate of grapes. Five minutes after that, Hank had won the first game.

"You're not concentrating," he accused.

"Who can concentrate? You're over there crunching away on the popcorn."

"Popcorn does not crunch. At least not a lot. It's hardly enough to distract a really good checkers player."

"I never said I was any good. Even Tommy can beat the socks off me. You're the one who wanted to play."

"I wanted to do something that would keep my mind off taking you to bed."

"Is it working?"

"No!"

"That's what I was afraid of. It's not working for me, either."

"Do you know why?"

"Physiologically or psychologically?" she inquired. He glared at her.

"It's because we're living here together, playing house, so to speak. Only we're not...you know." His voice trailed off weakly.

"See," she gloated. "You can't even talk about it."

"Do you honestly want to talk about it?"

"It's been my experience that talking usually helps."

Hank was shaking his head adamantly. "Not in this case. Take my word for it, Annie. Talking about sex will not get our minds off it."

"It might put it into perspective."

"Right now about the only thing that would put it into perspective for me is a cold shower, which I intend to take." He got as far as the door before turning back, a wistful expression on his face. "I don't suppose..."

"I am not taking the shower with you."

He grinned. "It was worth a shot."

The next morning they were both bleary-eyed and grouchy.

"What's wrong with you two?" Paul asked when they'd both snapped over something totally inconsequential.

"Not enough sleep," Hank said, staring pointedly at Ann.

"Whose fault was that?" she retorted, slamming a teacup down in front of him and pouring him some herbal tea.

"I want my soda," he said, pushing the cup aside.

"I threw them all out."

"You did what!" he bellowed, sounding like a wounded bear.

She smiled. "Try the tea."

"I will not drink this watered-down excuse for tea. There's no caffeine in it."

"That's the point."

In midargument Ann noticed that the kids were following the battle as if they were at a tennis match, looking back and forth, back and forth, as the barbs flew.

"Enough," she said with a sigh. "Truce."

"Does that mean I get my soda?" he inquired hopefully.

"It means we're going to stop fighting about it."

"We're only going to do that if one of them turns up on this table in the next ten seconds."

"Oh, go fly a kite!" she said and stalked out of the house. Openmouthed, the kids stared after her.

"Is Mom okay?" David asked hesitantly.

"She's fine," Hank said tersely.

"Are you sure?" David persisted.

Tracy shot a knowing look at Hank. "I think she's in love."

"Mom!" The chorus of voices was incredulous. Hank could feel his skin burn.

"Tracy, I don't think this is a topic that needs to be discussed just now."

"I'm right, aren't I?"

"Not now, Tracy."

Jason stared from one to the other before finally sending his chair flying as he got to his feet, scowling fiercely at Tracy. "You think Mom's in love with him? You're crazy! She's not out of her mind."

"Just because you and Hank don't get along doesn't mean Ann can't like him," Tracy retorted. "Don't be such a jerk."

"You're the jerk." He slammed out of the house.

"If you and Ann fall in love does that mean you'll be our dad?" Paul asked. "I think that'd be neat."

Hank felt as if he'd been punched in the gut. "Whoa, everybody. Let's slow down a minute. First of all, the way Ann and I feel is nobody's business but ours."

"Hey, we live here, too," Tracy protested.

"My point is that this is something she and I have to work out and we can't do that if you all are watching and questioning every move we make."

Tracy was nodding knowingly. Hank didn't trust that smug expression one bit. "You're in love all right."

"Tracy!"

She grinned unrepentantly. "Sorry. I got carried away. What can we do to help?"

"Keep your opinions and your guesswork to yourselves," he grumbled, knowing that was about as likely as shutting down the lurid speculation in the national tabloids. He began to have some sense of what celebrities went through when their personal lives got turned inside out in public.

As soon as the kids had all gone off to school, including Melissa, who was attending a nearby nursery school in the mornings, Hank left the house and walked slowly across the highway to Dolphin Reach, where Ann had her office. Though he knew all about the innovative treatment she was involved in there—it was where Todd had brought Kevin for help with his dyslexia—this was the first time he'd entered her professional domain.

A young receptionist looked up and smiled a harried greeting as she continued handling phone calls. When she was finally free, he asked for Ann's office.

"It's the second one on the left, but she's not there. I think she's down with the dolphins."

"Is she with a patient?"

"Nope. Her first one's not till ten."

"Thanks."

As he walked through the grounds and headed for the dock, his curiosity about her work mounted. What had ever given her the idea of using dolphins as a part of her psychological counseling? Then he spotted her at the end of a dock and thought he knew.

She was kneeling on a platform that stuck out into the protected harbor, her skirt swirling around her. A brisk wind tousled her hair. Dolphins surrounded her, their built-in smiles impossible to resist as they bobbed in the water. Seeing Ann's laughing response to their antics and knowing full well how troubled she'd been when she left the house, he began to see how the dolphins might be the perfect intermediary for a hard-to-reach patient.

"Annie."

Her laughter died at the sound of his voice and her gaze grew troubled. "Why are you here?"

"I thought we needed to talk."

"Not now. I'm busy."

"You don't have a patient scheduled for another hour. I'm booking this time."

"Sorry. I don't take clients with whom I have a personal involvement."

He grinned. "That won't work. You helped Kevin."

He saw her fighting a smile. "Okay, so I made one exception."

"Make another one."

"Why should I?"

"Because the kids just made me face up to something I've been avoiding."

Curiosity obviously overcame her reluctance to hear him out. "What's that?"

"I'm in love with you."

Ann looked stunned. And skeptical. But once the words were finally out of his mouth, Hank knew without a single lingering doubt that he meant them and that he would do anything he had to do to prove it to her. He dropped down beside her.

"Well?" he said finally.

"I don't know what to say."

"Aren't you supposed to say what you feel? That's what all those pop psychology books advise."

She searched his face for several long seconds before she finally spoke. "I think you're crazy."

"Now that's a nice professional analysis," he taunted, amused by what even he could recognize as denial. She didn't want it to be true, so therefore he was crazy.

"Don't make fun of me."

"I'm not. And, despite that panic I can see in your eyes, I'm not expecting you to admit that you're madly in love with me, either. I'm just letting you know where I stand."

"It won't work. You want to be in love with me because it would take away some of the guilt."

"What guilt? I haven't done anything to feel guilty about."

"But you want to."

"Annie, if mere lust doomed us all to hell, no one would ever get to heaven. I assure you I do not feel guilty for wanting you."

"What you really want is a short-term challenge. I can understand that. A man of your sexual appetites and past experience can hardly be blamed for following the same old predictable pattern."

Hank felt a sense of outrage building inside him. Here he was spilling his guts, admitting to an emotion he'd never expected to feel and he was getting dime-store psychoanalysis. He was tempted to pull her into his arms and kiss that silly, crooked mouth of hers until she couldn't come up with another ridiculous argument, but he had a hunch she would only see that as proving her point.

He reached over and ran his finger along her jaw, then down the pale column of her neck. He watched the pulse jump as his finger drifted onto her breast, circling and teasing until the peak was pebble hard. His eyes never left hers. Desire overcame doubts in their wary depths.

"What if this isn't a game?" he said, still caressing.

"Of course it is," she said in a choked whisper.

He leaned forward then and kissed her, very gently, holding himself back, making her want him as badly as he wanted her.

"But what if it's not, Annie?" he said when her breathing was ragged. "What then?"

With the question lingering to torment her, he stood and walked away.

Chapter Nine

Love? Hank Riley, the inveterate skirt chaser, was in love with her? No way. Uh-uh. Forget it. She doubted he even knew the definition of the word. Hell, she dealt with all sorts of permutations of love every single day and even she wasn't sure she'd recognize it when it hit her, so how could he be so sure?

Despite her denials, though, Hank's unexpected proclamation reverberated through Ann's head all day long. By the end of the afternoon, her patients—even the littlest ones—were beginning to ask her if *she* was okay.

The honest answer, of course, was a resounding no. It wasn't the one she gave them. She tried to concentrate on their problems, tried to work up some enthusiasm for the small successes she was seeing in their treatment, but all she could think about was Hank's crazy, impulsive, misguided declaration of love.

It was absolutely the last thing she'd expected him to say when he'd come chasing after her that morning. She'd thought, despite his innumerable flaws, that he was too honest, too straightforward to use powerful words like that as part of an obvious seduction technique. Besides, the man had to know he could get her into his bed anytime he wanted her there. That was part of the problem. She was willing. He wasn't. He seemed to have this crazy idea that he was protecting her by maintaining his physical distance, while he closed the emotional gap. At the rate he was going he would soon have her snared so tightly she'd never escape. Then when he realized his mistake, there'd be hell to pay—for both of them.

Well, it wasn't going to happen that way, she resolved. She wasn't interested in a commitment. She liked her life just the way it was. Taking care of six unruly, troubled children was more than enough to keep her life filled to overflowing. And, for all of his crazy protestations, she knew Hank was no more seriously interested in her than he was in having tea parties with Melissa and her dolls. Right now, living in their chaotic household was a novelty, but the fascination of family life would wear off soon enough. She was going to prove it to him.

That decided, she began to feel infinitely better. In fact, by the time she had dinner on the table, she was feeling downright cheerful and on top of things again. She felt in control.

Then Hank came in, smiled and her resolve melted. Just the sight of the man curled her toes. When he dropped a casual, husbandly kiss on her forehead, her knees went weak. When he lifted the lid on the pot of soup simmering on the stove and murmured some appreciative comment, she went all mushy inside. This was far more serious than she'd realized. What was happening to them? Hank was the one supposedly in love. She was simply coming unglued.

With five speculative faces looking on—plus Jason's sullen one—dinner was an uncomfortable affair. Hank did try his best to make everything seem perfectly normal. She had to give him that. She felt suddenly tongue-tied, while he asked all the right questions about school, doled out all the right bits of praise, saw that the after-dinner cleanup was organized. For a man who only weeks ago had been frozen solid at the mere thought of dealing with a bunch of children, he was doing awfully well. In fact, he was a natural. They might actually make a pretty good team.

"Hey, Mom," David said, drawing her attention away from her own chaotic thoughts. "Is what Hank said right? Are we all going to Miami next weekend?"

She blinked and stared at him. Where had that idea come from? She looked at Hank, who seemed particularly pleased with himself.

"We'll have to talk about it," she said evasively.

"I think it'd be really neat," Tracy said. "Just think of all the stores and movies to choose from."

"And the Miami Heat," Paul said of the basketball team. "Maybe they'll have a game. Could we go to that, Hank?"

"If Ann agrees," he said with unexpected and untimely deference.

She glared at him. While she'd been woolgathering, he'd gotten their hopes up. Now he'd tossed the ball into her court. The tactics were unfair, but effective. She'd been neatly trapped.

"If Hank doesn't mind taking all of you," she began, but he deftly put a stop to her one hope for a reprieve before she could even voice it.

"We'll *all* go," he said, watching her pointedly. "We can't go off and leave you here alone." It sounded very noble.

"Yeah, Mom," David concurred. "You need a vacation, too."

"Come on, Ann. It'll be better than a zillion miles of running," Tracy said. "You're always saying that even a little break is good for reducing stress."

Ann sighed in the face of all that well-calculated concern. She was even having her own advice thrown back at her. She supposed she ought to feel flattered that Tracy had even heard her. "We'll see. We'll have to check everybody's schedules to see when it would work out."

She glimpsed the triumphant look on Hank's face just as David said, "Oh, my gosh."

"What?" Ann said.

"The schedule. I almost forgot to tell you. There's a parents' night at school." He avoided looking directly at her when he asked, "Will you come?"

"Jeez, why do you care about a dumb old parents' night?" Jason said with derision. "All it is is a chance for the teachers to shoot off their mouths."

"Jason," Hank warned in a low voice.

Ann scowled at Jason as well. "If it's important to David, that's all that matters."

"Well, excuse me," Jason said, glaring at Hank and ignoring Ann. He took off without another word, knocking his chair into the counter in the process.

Hank looked ready to explode, but she managed to silence him with a slight shake of the head. For once, he actually listened to her. Ann vowed to have a talk with Jason later. In the meantime, though, she needed to reassure David, who was shifting in his chair, his expression embarrassed. He considered Jason to be the big brother he'd never had. Jason's criticism had obviously hurt. He looked as though he wished he'd never made the request.

"Never mind him. I'll be there," she promised, reaching for the family calendar she kept posted on the refrigerator. "When is it?"

"Day after tomorrow," he said, the enthusiasm gone from his voice.

"David!"

"I'm sorry. I forgot."

Ann knew better. He'd probably been afraid to bring it up before now. Although David had been with her a year now, he'd been shuttled through so many foster homes that he expected this one to be short-term as well. Despite her reassurances, he still wasn't convinced he had a permanent place in her heart. She ruffled his hair. "It's okay, sport. It's not a problem."

Hank stood. "Okay, guys, everybody scoot. You all have homework, I'm sure."

The kids scattered, but not before Tracy shot a knowing look at the two of them. Ann caught the thumbs-up signal she directed at Hank as she left.

"Nicely done," Ann said with an unmistakable edge of sarcasm.

He grinned unrepentantly. "Do you think they suspected I wanted to be alone with you?"

"Tracy certainly did. The others were probably just grateful that you let them off from doing the dishes."

He stared at the messy table in dismay. "Whoops. I knew there was something I'd forgotten." He stood and dropped a kiss on her cheek.

It was casual, she told herself. Perfectly meaningless.

It set off fireworks deep inside her.

"Don't worry," Hank was saying as she tried unsuccessfully to ignore the sparks he'd just ignited. "I'll get this parenthood stuff down before too long."

"Hank, we need to talk about this."

"About what?" he said with apparent innocence.

"Parenting," she said determinedly. "You and me. Trips to Miami."

"What about it?" he inquired as he ran water into the sink.

"Hank, will you pay attention to me, please?"

He gave her a wicked grin and swept her up and into his arms before she realized his intentions. "I'm delighted you finally asked."

"Hank!" she protested, trying to bite back a laugh.

"Yes?" he said, his tongue touching the shell of her ear and sending bolts of electricity shooting straight through her. Suddenly she no longer felt any desire to laugh.

"Are you ever serious?" she said with forced levity, trying to wriggle out of his embrace. If she gave in now, she had a feeling she'd be lost, that she'd never recapture her control of the situation.

"I am now," he murmured, demonstrating with a very serious, breath-stealing kiss. His lips were velvet fire against hers, persuasive. Her control slipped another notch.

"And I was this morning," he added.

She clung tenaciously to reality. "You were not. Now listen to me," she said, gasping when she felt his hands glide up and down her spine. He pressed kisses along her neck, lingering at the spots that drew tiny, unwilling gasps of pleasure.

"I am listening," he swore softly.

She brushed his hands away and backed off. "This is exactly what I mean. You're taking it for granted that I feel the same way you do."

"You do," he said with such confidence she wasn't sure whether to give in or hit him.

"I do not," she said with emphasis on each word, hoping they would penetrate that thick skull of his.

"Annie, you would not even consider going to bed with a man you didn't love. You are considering going to bed with me, ergo you're in love with me."

"You must have flunked logic."

"Actually, I did very well in it. I have a nice, tidy, scientific brain. I can reason things out with the best of them."

"This has nothing to do with reason."

"This what?"

"What we're talking about."

"You mean being in love?"

"Exactly."

"Well, I never said *that* made any sense. I just said it was a fact, a conclusion to be drawn from all the evidence."

"Go to hell."

"Annie, you're resorting to swearing again. Do you realize how often you do that when I'm winning an argument?"

"You are not winning this argument," she shouted at the top of her lungs, all pretense of calm gone.

He smirked—quite calmly, damn him—and went back to the sink. "That's what you think," he murmured, sounding very pleased with himself.

Ann slammed the back door on her way out.

The whole world was spinning out of control. Ann tried once more to put her feet on the floor, but it rocked and her stomach lurched. The ache in her head was exceeded only by the pains in her joints. All of them, including the little tiny ones in her toes. She fell back against the pillows, wondering just how badly her very green complexion contrasted with the pale blue sheets. All in all, she felt like hell. She didn't doubt for an instant that she probably looked ten times worse.

Glancing at the bedside clock, she groaned. David's parent-teacher night at school was starting in exactly two hours. She'd come home from work early to make sure that dinner was finished and out of the way before it was time to leave. She'd never made it past the bedroom, where she'd come to change her clothes.

What on earth was she going to do? She had to be there. She'd promised and David took promises very seriously, especially since no one had ever kept them until she'd come along.

"Mom, are you getting ready?" he shouted as he raced into her bedroom. At the sight of her, he skidded to a halt, his enthusiasm wilting.

"You're in bed," he said, his voice quivering with dismay. She saw him bravely fighting tears and her heart constricted, even as her stomach lurched.

"I'll be up in just a minute."

"But you look all funny, like you're really sick or something."

She tried not to groan at the understatement. Dying was closer to the mark, but she refused to discourage him any further. He was already looking crushed.

"You go get Tracy to iron a shirt for you and I'll be right in," she said with far more spirit than she'd ever figured to muster.

With a last skeptical look, he ran out the door, only to be replaced moments later by Hank. Ignoring his concerned expression, she struggled to her feet and promptly felt another wave of nausea wash through her.

"Oh, God," she moaned, bracing herself against the nightstand.

"Annie love, get back into bed." Hank's tone cajoled, the way it might an obstinate child.

"I can't." She did, however, compromise by sitting down on the edge. Just for a minute. Just until the room stopped spinning.

Hank strolled purposefully toward her, lifted a corner of the top sheet and pointed. "In!"

She resented the domineering tone, but arguing was beyond her. She simply shook her head.

He looked disgusted and sounded furious as he muttered something about her lousy temperament. "Hell, woman, you're a doctor. You should know better."

"I have a Ph.D. in psychology," she pointed out with another burst of contrariness. "Not an M.D."

"All the more reason for you to be using a little common sense. Even if going tonight doesn't kill you, it will spread your germs through the entire population of the Keys. I doubt anyone, including David, would thank you for that."

"But I can't let him down," she protested. She was wavering, though. What Hank said made perfect sense, but then Hank wasn't a mother. "I don't think anyone's ever gone to a parent-teacher night for him before. Can't you see how much it means?"

"Of course I can understand that. Put your head down, Annie," he tempted.

She ran her fingers over the pillow. The percale material felt very cool, very comforting. Her skin was burning up. If only...

"I'll go." Hank's announcement interrupted her mental debate.

She stared at him in openmouthed astonishment. "You?"

He grinned. "Yeah. What's so weird about that? Can't you picture me in those tiny little chairs?"

At the moment, she was having trouble picturing anything through the feverish haze of this blasted flu. Of all the times to pick up a bug. She never got sick. She was healthy as an ox. She ate oat bran and fresh vegetables and took her vitamins. Hank was the one who ought to be deathly ill.

"After all, if I'm going to be a part of this family, then it's time I took on more of the responsibilities," Hank was saying. Something in the comment alarmed her, but she couldn't think clearly enough to pinpoint it. "I'm sure David won't mind. How about it?"

"Go," she murmured finally.

With great effort, she swung her leaden legs back onto the bed and fell back against the pillows. Hank settled her more comfortably, his touch gentle as he awkwardly tucked the sheet around her and plumped the pillows. He vanished at once, only to return in what seemed like seconds with a glass of juice and a pitcher of ice water.

"They always tell you to drink plenty of fluids with this stuff," he said. He sounded very matter-of-fact, as if he'd played nursemaid to dozens of women. The idea bothered her more than she cared to admit.

"So drink," he urged.

Ann nodded. The very thought made her insides revolt. "In a minute."

"Now," he ordered, much less compassionately. He held a straw to her lips and waited until she'd swallowed several sips of the water. When she had, he placed everything within easy reach, then stood back and surveyed his handiwork, his expression troubled. "Are you going to be okay until I get back?"

She gave a weak nod.

"Tracy's taking care of the little ones. She'll feed them and get them to bed. They won't bother you. She'll check on you later and I'll be home in no time to make sure you're okay. If you need anything in the meantime, shout."

The idea amused her. She barely had enough strength to whisper. "No shouting," she murmured sleepily, wondering at the unexpected feeling of contentment that was stealing over her. No one ever fussed over her, took care of her. Not until Hank. With him, it was getting to be a habit. Again the idea was somehow troubling, but she didn't have the will to try to figure out why.

"No shouting, huh?" he said, chuckling. "That'll be a pleasant change. I'm sorry I'm not going to be around for it."

His teasing words faded out. For an instant she was certain she felt the light brush of his beard on her cheek, the touch of his lips, but she knew she had to be wrong. Not even Hank Riley would take advantage of a woman when she was on her deathbed.

Ann awoke to sunlight streaming in the bedroom window. She lay perfectly still, testing her body, waiting for the first ache to make its presence felt. She waited several minutes. She felt…okay. Not ready for wind sprints, but intact and human.

Just as she was about to test the sensation by crawling out of bed, the door swung open and Hank came in bearing a tray.

"Well, it's about time you woke up," he said with the sort of forced cheer generally reserved for hospital rooms and uttered by nurses who thought of their patients as dimwits. It more or less suited the way Ann was feeling, slightly off kilter and out of control.

"What time is it?"

"Nearly noon."

Her eyes snapped wide and she struggled to a sitting position. "Good heavens, the kids! What about school?"

With disgustingly little effort, Hank shoved her back. "They've gone. Not a one of them was late. Their clothes could have been a little neater, but I'm lousy with an iron. Feel like some tea and toast? I fixed some earlier, but I didn't want to wake you. By now you probably need it."

She regarded him warily. In her weakened condition, she figured a little caution was called for. "Why aren't you at work?"

"I've been. I came back to check on you."

"I'm better. You can go now."

"Here's your hat, what's your hurry," he mocked.

She flushed guiltily and fiddled with the sheet, trying unobtrusively to get it above the neckline of what she'd just realized was a practically transparent, very sexy nightgown. She didn't exactly remember getting into it. She decided it was best not to ask how it had happened or who had chosen it. She usually wore oversize T-shirts to bed. This had been one of those crazy impulse buys on a day when she'd been feeling down and had needed to remind herself of her femininity. She'd never worn it.

"Sorry," she murmured, not meeting his gaze. "I just don't want to take you away from your job when it's not necessary."

"They can manage without me for a while," he said matter-of-factly, settling down beside her on the bed. He acted as though he belonged there. She suddenly felt feverish again. He held out the cup of tea. "Drink this."

She ignored the tea. She was less successful in ignoring his proximity. "Really," she said, running her fingers through her hair. She could tell it was sticking straight out in every direction. "I can manage."

"I'm sure you can, but why don't you relax for five minutes and let me wait on you."

She met his gaze and saw something there that made her breath catch in her throat. He looked as though bringing her tea and toast was important to him in some unfathomable way. He looked every bit as confused by the need as she felt by her reaction to it. He also looked determined. She recognized that pigheaded expression and gave up the fight.

"Thanks," she said finally, her breath uneven. She took the cup and sipped. He'd made the raspberry tea. He'd even remembered to leave out the sugar. "It's wonderful."

"Now the toast," he coaxed.

"I'm not so sure . . ."

"Try it. You should be able to keep it down and you need something in your stomach."

She took the smallest bite possible, just to satisfy him. "How'd last night go?" she asked, hoping to get his attention away from her continued lack of appetite.

"Fine. David's teacher had nothing but good things to say about his work. She says he's improved tremendously in the time he's been with you."

"How'd you explain your presence?"

"I said we were living together."

Ann choked on the tea. "You what!" Her eyes widened in alarm.

He grinned without the slightest hint of remorse. "I tried not to leer when I said it, though."

She moaned. "Hank Riley, are you determined to ruin my reputation?"

"Annie, my love, your reputation is already well established. That's why I said it."

"I beg your pardon."

He chuckled. "You're known for taking in strays. Surely one more won't make a difference."

"Most of my strays have been under the age of twelve, at least when they arrived. Jason was a little older, but then nobody would ever think that he... None of them have been so..." She was at a loss for words that wouldn't give away exactly how he affected her.

"Decidedly masculine?" he offered with a smug expression.

She laughed, despite herself. "You never let up, do you?"

"Of course not. Why on earth would I do that, especially on a rare occasion when I have you weak and at my mercy."

"I am not weak."

"Care to prove it?" he challenged, leaning toward her.

"Go away," she muttered, shoving the tray at him with enough force to rattle the teapot.

"Ungrateful woman," he taunted, taking the tray. "We'll finish this discussion later."

"Don't count on it," she said, suddenly feeling drained.

"Ah, Annie, you really should stop fighting me. It's such a wasted effort."

"Not in this lifetime," she murmured, yawning.

She couldn't seem to keep her eyes open another second, not even when Hank whispered, "Happy Valentine's Day, sweetheart," and folded her fingers around a small package.

Once again she was almost certain she felt the gentle touch of his lips as she drifted off into a dreamless, contented sleep.

Chapter Ten

It was the hard imprint of a box pressing into her cheek and the subtle crackling of paper that woke Ann later that afternoon. Opening her eyes reluctantly she found a package on her pillow. She only dimly recalled Hank putting it into her hand. Wrapped in silver paper, it had now-crushed streamers of red ribbon and clusters of tiny white hearts.

Valentine's Day.

Suddenly she remembered his whispered wish as she'd fallen asleep. Her heart thumped unsteadily as she picked the package up and studied it. The box was long and narrow and flat. There was a slight rustling sound when she shook it gently. It could be a gold pen, but somehow she doubted it. The prospect of what it might be made her very nervous. She didn't want Hank giving her jewelry. It seemed too personal, too important, too committed. Especially on Valentine's Day.

"Open it," Hank said, suddenly appearing in the doorway.

The low rasp of his voice set her ablaze. The significance of the package fanned the flames. "I'm not sure I should."

"Why not?"

"I don't think you ought to be giving me presents."

Blue eyes twinkled back, his expression a mixture of amusement and indignation. "Who made you guardian angel over my finances?"

She glared at him as desire ebbed, replaced by more familiar irritation. She hated it when he decided to be deliberately obtuse. "I am not worried about your finances. You know what I mean."

"You mean you are not in the habit of accepting gifts from men."

It sounded a little silly when he said it. It was also an understatement. The last time she'd received a Valentine's card from a male she had been in the sixth grade. "Something like that."

"Maybe you should get used to it. You deserve presents, Annie. And I intend to see that you get them. Now open this one before I have to remind you that learning to receive is as important as learning to give."

He had a point. She had been behaving ungraciously. It was only a small gift, after all. Unexpected excitement bubbled up inside her as she gently removed the ribbon. She was picking carefully at the tape, trying to prolong the anticipation, when Hank groaned and took the package from her.

"That's no way to open a present," he said. "This is how you open it."

He grabbed an edge of the paper and gave one quick rip. Grinning, he handed her the box.

"My way gives you more time to savor it," she grumbled as she caressed the velvet covering.

"Sorry. I'm not a patient man."

"So I've noticed." She snapped open the box before he could take over that as well. With trembling fingers, she lifted away the tissue paper inside. Nestled on the satin lining was a sparkling diamond heart dangling from a delicate gold chain.

Her own heart filled to overflowing with all sorts of unexpected emotions. She lifted her gaze to meet Hank's. "I've never had anything so beautiful."

He touched the diamond with a finger that seemed to shake. "It's mine, Annie," he said in a low voice that tugged at her senses. "The heart is mine and now you have it."

Tears glistened in her eyes and clogged her throat as she whispered, "Oh, Hank."

"Do you really like it?"

"I'll treasure it always," she said, fumbling with the clasp. Hank took the necklace from her and settled it around her neck. His fingers followed the chain of gold from her nape to the hollow at the base of her throat where the heart now nestled, warmed by her skin and fired by his touch.

Maybe it was just her weakened condition or maybe it was the magic of the traditional lovers' holiday, but with Hank gazing so tenderly into her eyes, Ann almost believed in love.

For the life of her, Ann couldn't remember actually agreeing to go to Miami. On Friday afternoon, though, she came home to find that each of the kids had a bag packed and that they were all in the living room waiting for her. They looked so excited, she didn't have the heart to protest. After a heated competition, Paul and Tommy won the right to ride with Hank on the trip up. Everyone else piled into her station wagon.

"Now you're sure you understand the directions?" Hank asked for the tenth time as he closed the door of the car. "I don't want you getting lost."

"Hank, it is a straight drive up U.S. 1. How could I possibly get lost?"

"Okay. Just remember, if we get separated in traffic, I'll wait for you at the Suniland Shopping Center at One Hundred and Twelfth Street. I'll park in front of the grocery store. Finding my place in Coconut Grove is a little confusing. I want to lead you in from there."

"And if I get ahead of you?" she teased.

"You won't," he said with that familiar confident wink.

Before she could react, he walked away. She stared after him. As his taunt sank in, she was suddenly seized by doubts.

"Hank Riley, you be careful how you drive with my children in your truck," she shouted. He waved back cheerfully.

"What are we going to do in Miami?" Tracy asked as they pulled out onto the highway. Ann smiled at the excitement in Tracy's voice. More and more the past few days, her mood was lightening and she was allowing her natural exuberance to show. The barriers were slowly falling away. She'd even told Ann all about the date that had gone awry the night she'd called Hank in Miami. Ann knew she had Hank to thank for that. He'd been encouraging Tracy to be more open with her and Tracy was listening, as she did to everything Hank said. She clearly idolized the man, though Ann was no longer worried that Tracy might be suffering from a crush. She'd made it all too plain that she was encouraging a match between Ann and Hank.

"This is Hank's adventure," Ann told her. "We'll just have to see what he has planned when we get there."

The possibilities made her increasingly anxious. She hated the long, tedious drive, hated the faster pace of Miami, worried about the crime and wasn't crazy about allowing her children loose in that environment. She also had this nagging feeling that Hank's patience was at an end and that he was plotting something for the two of them. That very nearly panicked her. It was what she'd claimed to want, but now she felt uncertain, as if taking that next step in their relationship would commit them to a direction in which she wasn't at all prepared to go with her life.

"Well, I want to go shopping," Tracy said.

"Me, too," Melissa said.

"I've been saving up for a new outfit." Tracy looked over at Ann, suddenly sounding shy. "Would you help me pick it out? You always look so great. You have your own sense of style. You don't just follow everybody else.''

Feeling as though her heart would burst at the compliment, Ann smiled back. "I'd love to help you find something really special. With your coloring, you can wear all the hot new colors that are in this year. You don't know how lucky you are."

"Who cares about shopping?" David protested. "I want to go to the basketball game and eat a dozen hot dogs."

"Me, too," Melissa chimed in, bouncing excitedly in her car seat.

Ann chuckled. "What about you, Jason?"

"I don't see why we have to go at all."

"Aren't you excited about any of the things you could do in Miami?" she persisted.

"I've been there. It's no big deal."

"When did you ever go to Miami?" Tracy scoffed.

"Me and some guys went a couple of years ago, smart mouth."

"Sure."

"We did. It's not so hot. Just a lot of people. I like it better in the Keys."

"Well, don't let Hank hear you say that," Tracy warned. "You'll hurt his feelings."

"Nothing would hurt that guy's feelings. He's about as sensitive as a block of cement."

"Jason," Ann said very quietly, deciding things had gone far enough. "Hank wants this weekend to be special for all of you. Can't you at least try to meet him halfway?"

The request was met by silence. Ann sighed. Fortunately Melissa, Tracy and David more than made up for Jason's lack of enthusiasm. David made sporadic attempts to get Jason to talk about what he'd seen on his last trip to Miami, but eventually even he gave up and let Jason sulk.

Despite his teasing challenge about his driving speed, Hank never got too far ahead of them. She followed more closely as he led them off Dixie Highway and into Coconut Grove. Ann recognized part of the route. It was the same way she had gone to see Liz after she and Todd had married. There was something wild and seductive about the dense foliage, the spread of banyan trees and thick undergrowth. Despite their proximity, the houses maintained their privacy. Although she preferred the wide expanses of sky and water in the Keys, the intimate atmosphere here had a certain primitive appeal to it that made her blood begin to race. It stirred fantasies of jungle adventures and sensual romance.

When Hank turned into a driveway that was practically hidden, she had to swallow hard against the strong emotions that were stirring in her. She felt like the uncertain heroine in some Gothic novel first arriving at the mysterious, secluded mansion of the hero, wondering what was in store for her future. She turned off the engine and sank back in the seat, trying to regain her composure as the kids scrambled from the car.

"Annie," Hank said quietly. Her guilty gaze shot up to meet his questioning eyes. "Are you okay?"

"Just fine," she said with forced bravado, getting out of the car. "The kids were wondering what you had planned for the weekend."

"Tonight I thought we'd go to Bayside for dinner and a little shopping, then to the Miami Heat game at the arena. How does that sound?"

"Busy."

He laughed, then kissed her soundly. "We'll find time just for us. I promise."

She flushed as her pulse ran wild. "That's not what I meant."

"Maybe not," he said with another of those damnable winks. "But I meant it just the same. Now come on in and let me show you around."

The house was spectacular. Ann recognized Todd's architectural touch: clean lines, wide sweeps of glass and cool, Spanish-style tiles and stucco walls. There was a huge fireplace in the living room.

Amused, she glanced at Hank. "In Miami?"

He grinned. "It's the one thing I've always envied from northern winters. It's worth it on the few nights a year here when it's cold enough to use it." He slid his arms around her waist. "It's also very romantic, don't you think?"

Her heartbeat skipped at the seductive look in his eyes. An image of a dozen different women sipping wine in front of that fireplace made her shiver. As if he'd read her thoughts, his embrace tightened. "Never before, Annie."

She gazed up at him disbelievingly.

"I swear it," he said. "I know you think I've been quite a rake. To be perfectly honest, there's some truth to my reputation, but there's never been anyone in my life I cared about enough to bring into my home. When I come here, it's my retreat from the world.''

Ann wanted very much to believe him, especially when his mouth covered hers persuasively. What began as subtle pressure quickly turned to hard, demanding hunger. All those feelings of warmth and contentment that she'd begun experiencing in the past few weeks swept through her as his tongue invaded. The deep, drugging power of the kiss claimed her, leaving her knees trembling and her head spinning. Hank's strong hands were splayed on her hips, pulling her close. Fit tightly against him, her body ached with longing. Heat flared, white-hot, all-consuming heat.

''I want you so badly, Annie. Feel what you do to me,'' he said, pressing her hand against him. She pulled away, but like the moth drawn inevitably toward the flame, she was drawn back, fascinated by the evidence of her power over him. When he shuddered at the gentle sweep of her touch, her eyes shot to his face in wonder.

''We're going to be good together, Annie. I know you're still afraid, but I'm going to convince you just how right this is. Before the weekend's out, I'm going to make you mine.''

The vow made her knees go weak again. The unspoken *forever* behind it made her heart pound so hard against her ribs, she thought she'd die from it. How had a man so wrong for her gotten to her so completely? How had he evaded her defenses, overcome her common sense and landed smack in the middle of her heart?

Thank goodness for chaperons, she thought as the sound of running footsteps intruded on their moment of privacy. She backed out of the embrace, her cheeks flaming with color. Hank seemed unfazed by the throbbing passion that had sparked between them. She saw that ability to distance himself so rapidly as more evidence of his jaded past and it renewed her qualms. He turned to the children with a perfectly calm look on his face. One arm, however, remained tightly curved around her waist as a determined reminder of what they'd just shared.

"So did you all pick out your rooms?" he asked.

"This place is really neat," Paul said. "You gotta see it, Mom. There must be dozens and dozens of rooms."

Hank laughed at the enthusiasm. "Not quite that many, but enough for this crowd."

"There's a pool, too," David said.

"And one of those romantic hot tub things," Tracy chimed in, casting a pointed look at Ann.

Ann did not want to hear about hot tubs, not when her body was still quivering with unfulfilled expectations. She looked hurriedly at Hank. "Isn't it time we left for dinner?"

His amusement at her frantic appeal apparent, he nodded. "Okay, is everybody ready to get moving?"

He outlined the plans for the night. As she'd anticipated, they were met with wholehearted approval. The one thing he failed to mention was exactly when he intended to carry out his seduction of her. Though she was more than grateful for the omission, it left her with anticipation sizzling through her bloodstream. Visions of that hot tub danced through her head with all the dazzling temptation of Christmas sugar plums.

Anticipation, she noted with surprise. Not panic. What on earth was happening to her? Surely she couldn't actually be falling in love with the man.

But she was, she admitted candidly as she watched his enthusiasm at the basketball game. Since she had no idea what was happening on the court and didn't particularly care, she allowed herself to indulge her desire to watch Hank, to study the way he interacted with each of the children in a way that was uniquely thoughtful. He was crazy and indulgent, but he was also firm. He was interested, without fawning over them. Even with Jason, he kept his temper in check, ignoring the sullen silences and continuing to make occasional efforts to make the boy feel part of the family fun.

On the way home, the younger kids fell asleep in the car, while Tracy, David and Paul continued to chatter about the game and the plans for the next day.

"I was thinking about the Coconut Grove Art Festival," Hank said. "How does that sound?"

"Art, yuck," Paul protested.

"It's outdoors," Hank countered. "There will be music and lots of food."

"I guess that'd be okay," Paul relented.

"Sounds terrific to me," Tracy said.

"Then in the afternoon, Liz and Todd have invited us over to their house for a barbecue."

Ann gazed at him, surprised. "When did this happen?"

"I talked to them earlier in the week."

"I see," she said stiffly as they arrived at the house. Fortunately the kids took off for bed before the argument she anticipated could explode.

"What's wrong?" Hank asked the minute they were alone. He took her hand and idly drew provocative circles on her sensitive palm.

"Nothing," she snapped, trying to tug her hand away. He held tight. "Why should anything be wrong?"

"I haven't the vaguest idea, but something obviously is."

"Liz and Todd are my friends," she began, only to go silent at the justifiably amazed expression on Hank's face.

"They're my friends, too," he reminded her gently, effectively dashing her anger. He kissed her palm, his tongue hot and moist against her flesh. "Todd is my partner. Now what's this really all about?"

She sighed heavily. "I'm sorry. That was a dumb thing to say. I guess it just threw me that all these plans were made without my knowledge."

Hank drew her down on the sofa beside him and settled her against the curve of his shoulder. "Annie, you've been sick all week. I didn't want to bother you with the details. Besides, I wanted to make the plans. I wanted this to be a real vacation for you. If I know you, you'd have filled the little time we have with trips to bookstores to pick up the latest psychology books."

She managed a feeble grin. "I still plan to do exactly that," she retorted with a teasing defiance. "And I've promised Tracy a shopping trip for a new outfit. Maybe we'll take it after we leave Liz and Todd's."

Hank shook his head adamantly. "I've planned for your shopping trip. We'll stop at the mall down in Cutler Ridge on the way home on Monday."

"Monday? Hank, the kids have school on Monday. I have patients."

"The kids do not have school. It's the President's Day holiday. As for you, you only had one appointment on your calendar and I was able to get the receptionist over at Dolphin Reach to rearrange it."

"Dammit, Hank, you had no right," she said, pulling away from him. He was taking over her life, managing it with the same precision that he brought to his building projects. She couldn't allow it. "We're going back on Sunday."

"Annie, calm down. Why should we waste a day?"

He sounded incredibly patient. "Don't you patronize me, you muscle-bound cretin," she snapped back. "I will not calm down. And we'll go back on Sunday because I say so."

"Muscle-bound cretin? I like that," he said, chuckling. "If you really want to insist on going back on Sunday and disappointing the kids, then we'll go back on Sunday."

The ease with which he twisted things around to make her the bad guy exasperated her. His refusal to take offense only infuriated her more. She was really spoiling for a good fight and he was turning agreeable on her. She'd hoped a royal battle would take away this tension that was building inside her. Maybe it would take her mind off her desire to be in Hank's arms, in his bed.

"Damn you, Hank."

He shook his head. "Tsk, tsk. There you go again. You're swearing."

"Oh, go to hell."

"Annie, Annie, the children."

"The kids are all in bed," she mumbled, defeated by his teasing.

"And that makes it okay? I'm surprised at you, Annie."

"You are the most impossible..."

"Lovable?"

"*Impossible* man I have ever met."

"But you love me."

"I do not love you."

He pulled her into his lap and kissed her thoroughly. When she could gather her senses, she opened her eyes and met his satisfied smirk. "Liar," he whispered softly, then claimed her lips again. This time she didn't even pretend to struggle. She only sighed and whispered, mostly to herself, "If I am, then God help me."

The Coconut Grove Art Festival was not an event Ann would have expected Hank to enjoy. In fact, she had thought that even she would find the traffic jams irritating, the huge crowds tiresome and the art little more than junk. She was wrong on all counts. First of all, they were able to walk from his house, avoiding the bumper-to-bumper lines of cars. Once there, Hank clung firmly to her hand and tugged her from one display to another with all the enthusiasm of a kid in a candy store.

"Come on, Annie," he urged more than once. "You have to see this."

He pulled her to a booth filled with huge oil paintings. She studied the landscapes painted in the Everglades. They captured the barren vastness, but none of the majesty.

"Sorry. I don't like them," she said, keeping her voice low and turning away from the artist who sat nearby.

"Why not?"

"There's no emotion in them. The Everglades are unique, special. In these paintings, they look ordinary."

He stepped back and looked more closely. "You may have a point. You have a good eye."

She opened her mouth, but he touched a finger to her lips. "Don't you dare say you only know what you like."

She laughed. "I was not going to say that. I was going to tell you that I used to write an art column for my college paper."

"Oh," he said meekly.

His humble deference lasted another thirty seconds before he was touting the virtues of another craftsman a few booths away. "Look at this jewelry. What do you think?"

"It's lovely," she said distractedly, barely looking at the bold silver pieces that she normally would have loved.

"You're not even looking."

"Where are the kids?"

"Across the street, three booths down."

She looked in the direction in which he'd pointed. They were all there, every one of them. She counted just to be sure.

"I'm not going to let them get lost, Annie," he said quietly, tilting her chin up so he could look directly into her eyes. "I promise."

"Okay, so I get a little crazy."

"You're a mother."

"Yes. I am." She said it as though she was trying to make a point, but with Hank staring tenderly into her eyes, she lost track of the message she'd had in mind.

Just then they were joined by the kids. "Can we get some ice cream?" Paul pleaded.

"I want 'ade," Melissa said.

Hank turned deliberately to Jason. "You know where the food booths are, son?"

"I saw 'em."

"Then you make sure that everyone stays to- gether," he said, handing over some money. "Meet us on the corner in a half hour."

Jason seemed startled by the gesture. Ann caught a fleeting look of pride in his eyes before he hid it be- hind his usual moody mask. "Come on, guys," he said, sounding put-upon.

"I'm not sure that was such a good idea," she said worriedly. "Shouldn't we go with them?"

"Tracy's with them, too, and he has to learn that we do trust him."

"But you don't," she countered. "You've said all along that he was heading for trouble."

"I know and I still think that's possible, but we've got to do everything we can to head it off. I thought the job would help, but it hasn't."

"I think it has. He won't let you see it, but he seems more self-confident. The responsibility has been good for him."

"Annie, he's not accepting the responsibility," he blurted, then immediately looked as though he wished he could retract the words. Ann's heart sank.

"At least not the way I'd hoped he would," he amended hurriedly.

"What do you mean?"

Hank sighed. "Let's talk about this later."

"We'll talk about it now."

"Annie . . ."

She finally lost patience and snapped, "Hank, just tell me. What's wrong?"

"He hasn't been coming in to work."

"Why on earth not? What does he say about it?"

"Ted says he's had an excuse every time. Not terribly legitimate ones, but he has been calling in, which I suppose is something."

"Haven't you confronted him about it?"

"No. He reports to Ted. For the time being, I'm staying out of it. If he gets fired as a result of his behavior, it may do him good to realize that there are consequences."

"Dammit, Hank, you should have told me about this. I would have talked to him."

"A boss doesn't go running to Mother when an employee acts up. Besides, I didn't want to upset you."

"Well, I am upset."

"Exactly." He took her by the shoulders and turned her to face him. The crowds continued to mill around them, but as far as Ann was concerned it was just the two of them—and Jason.

She sighed. What would it have been like to have met Hank at a time in her life when she was totally free of responsibilities, when she would have been free to get to know him without all the pressures they faced now? Well, she thought with a pragmatic shrug, there was no point in wondering about that. As Hank liked to remind her, this was the hand they'd been dealt. They either had to fold or play it out. Since Hank seemed unlikely to drop out, she wouldn't, either.

"We are not going to let this spoil this vacation," he insisted now. "We have three days up here..."

"Two."

"Whatever. There will be plenty of time after that to decide what to do about Jason. For now we are all going to enjoy ourselves. Understand?"

"Just like that?" she said with a skeptical snap of her fingers.

His eyes twinkled with amusement. "Just like that."

"Well, since you seem to be in charge, then I suppose we'll just have to follow orders." She caught the glint of satisfaction in his eyes and hastily amended, "For the moment."

"Your submissiveness is duly noted."

"Enjoy it while it lasts," she said dryly as the kids caught up with them.

"Oh, I intend to," he said, his gaze locking with hers.

After another hour of browsing, Hank declared it was time to move on to Liz and Todd's.

"Yes, captain," she said, giving him a jaunty salute.

He leaned down to whisper, "Watch it, lady. You can be court-martialed for that kind of disrespect to an officer."

"And the punishment?"

He slid his hand up her side until it rested just below the curve of her breast. "I have several things in mind," he said, his expression very serious. Ann's heart thumped unsteadily.

"Shall I enumerate?" he asked huskily.

Caught up by the expression in his eyes and the rasp in his voice, she could only shake her head. Hank responded with another of those slow, deliberate winks, then blithely walked off, leading the family back to the car. Ann had to jerk herself out of the sensual torpor he'd left her in.

At Liz and Todd's she was hardly aware of the food or the activity that swirled around them. She responded to Liz's curious questions with what she hoped were rational answers, but she couldn't seem to focus on anything other than Hank as he played touch football with the whole gang on the front lawn. Even David had been persuaded to join in and after an initial hesitation, he was now wholeheartedly engaged in the competition. Just more evidence of Hank's magic, she thought.

"Interesting," Liz observed, sitting down beside her on the grass.

"Hmm." She blinked and turned to her friend. "What?"

"You seem awfully absorbed in the game."

"Hmm."

"Or is it one of the players you're attracted to?"

"Hmm."

"Ann!" Liz said in exasperation.

She dragged her attention away from the sight of Hank in jeans and T-shirt sprawled on the ground under a whole gang of giggling children. They were tickling him, which she didn't recall as a traditional tactic in the game. Still, he seemed to be enjoying it thoroughly. She caught herself smiling.

"Ann!"

She dragged her attention back to Liz. "What?"

"What's going on between you and Hank?"

"Nothing."

"Oh, really. I find that difficult to believe. He's a very attractive man. You've been living under the same roof for weeks now. Surely there are sparks of some kind."

Sparks? There was a veritable forest fire. She was not ready to admit it.

"You know for a psychologist who touts the healing virtues of communication, you're awfully quiet. Do you have any idea how frustrating that is?"

She turned a baleful look on Liz. "And you, my friend, are treading on thin ice."

Liz chuckled as she got to her feet. "Gee, you seem to be in about the same state Hank was in when he was here for dinner a couple of weeks ago. I can't tell you how glad I am that it's all working out."

"Working out? Nothing is working out," she said adamantly as Liz went back inside. Ann strode purposefully after her. She had to straighten her out before she got some crazy notion in her head. "Did you hear me? Nothing is working out. Do not gloat. Do not get your hopes up. Nothing is working out."

"Hmm," Liz said.

The noncommittal reply set Ann's teeth on edge. "Aren't you going to say anything?"

Liz returned her gaze innocently. "I think you've just said it all."

"Oh, go to hell," she snapped, just in time for Hank to hear her. He pulled her into a casual hug.

"There she goes again," he said to Liz. "Has she always had this tendency to swear when she gets upset?"

"I wouldn't know. I've never seen her upset before."

"Interesting," he commented, never taking his eyes from hers. "Very interesting."

"Leave me alone," she growled.

He shook his head. "Come with me."

"Where?" she asked suspiciously.

"Do you have to question every little thing? Just come."

Something in his voice told her not to argue. With a last look back at Liz, who was grinning broadly, she went with Hank. Outside, he led her to the car and urged her inside.

"Hank, we can't leave," she protested even as a sweet tension began to build inside her.

"Oh, yes, we can."

"The kids..."

"Will be just fine. Liz is a teacher. She's used to handling more kids than this."

"But they're going to think we're terribly rude."

"I assure you that is not what they're going to think."

Her eyes widened. "Hank, exactly what did you tell them?"

"The truth, that I wanted to be alone with you."

"And they went along with it?"

He gave a secretive little smile. "Let's just say they owed me one."

Ann folded her hands tightly in her lap and stared straight ahead. "Hank, I am not ready for this."

"Annie, believe me, we are both more than ready for this. Before the afternoon is out I'm going to prove it."

"But that's just it, it's afternoon."

"Late afternoon." He peered at her. "You have something against making love in the afternoon?" he teased.

Well, there it is, she thought wildly. The words were out in the open, lying there between them like a gauntlet that had been thrown down. "It all seems so calculated somehow," she retorted.

"Annie, we are living with six children. I can almost guarantee you that making love would have to be calculated under circumstances like that."

She regarded him closely. "Doesn't that bother you? Isn't spontaneity better?"

His voice dropped to a seductive murmur. "Annie, I want you in my arms. That's the only thing that matters."

She swallowed hard as he continued. "I want to kiss every single inch of you. I want to get to know your body as well as I know my own. I want to bring you alive under my fingers. If I have to do a little calculating to accomplish that, I can handle it." He turned his head toward her. "Can you?"

"I don't know," she said honestly, though her heart was beating so hard and fast she could barely hear herself think.

He reached over and took her clenched hands in his. "Annie, once we get there, once we're inside and all alone, if this isn't right for you, we'll forget it. I promise. Okay?"

She heard the raw hunger in his voice, saw the depth of desire in his eyes and still she recognized the sincerity of the promise. Hank would be guided by her needs. What she wanted would always be uppermost in his mind.

Suddenly the last of her doubts fled, replaced by a wild, pounding urgency she'd never thought to experience. Responding to that frantic need, she lifted his hand to her lips and kissed the scarred knuckles, the callused palm. She felt the shudder that gripped him at her touch and asked softly, "Think you can drive any faster without getting caught?"

Chapter Eleven

One of the few advantages of winter, Ann decided, was that darkness came early. She was grateful for the rapidly dimming light because the minute they walked through the front door of Hank's house, her timidity returned. The twilight shadows helped her to hide her fears from Hank, though they did nothing to keep them from her heart.

Even though a part of her yearned desperately to be in Hank's arms, wanted to know the sheer physical pleasure of abandoning herself to his possession, another part was still holding back. She was still deeply troubled by the cold planning of it, worried even more about the long-term consequences for her emotions. The risks seemed enormous, far too great for a woman who'd only gambled on love once and lost everything.

They'd barely made it into the living room when Hank said, "I'm a mess from the football game. I think I'll take a shower."

He said it matter-of-factly, as if there were nothing more important on his mind than washing away a little dirt and grass. The comment was so far from the romantic murmurings she'd been anticipating, Ann felt like laughing hysterically with relief. Then she felt like screaming. If they were going to make love, why couldn't they just do it and get it over with? Why this slow torture, when they'd already waited far too long? She hadn't felt this nervous the first time...the only other time.

"Hank," she began, intending to protest, only to have him take her hand and squeeze it gently.

"Come with me," he suggested softly, his gaze locked with hers.

Heat pulsed through her, quick and hard and thrilling. Excitement and that maddening, intense desire warred with caution. "I don't know..."

"You can scrub my back."

It was a light, almost innocent taunt, but the prospect of touching him, of running her fingers over his shoulders set her blood on fire. The temptation was irresistible. Further denial would have been as pointless as trying to hold back the tides.

Willing herself not to think beyond the moment, she went with him through the house to the master bedroom suite. The previous night she had avoided this end of the house, not daring to envelop herself in the intimacy of Hank's room. She'd been afraid to enter a room that was so very much his domain. Now she gazed around with rapt curiosity.

The carpeting was a thick, dark navy. The bed was king-size, the only size large enough to accommodate a man of Hank's stature. Staring at it made her pulse race. The comforter was a rich, masculine pattern of navy and beige, the lines of all the furniture clean and modern. Vertical blinds let in the last of the muted afternoon light and shadowed images of the garden beyond the sliding glass doors. It was expensive, understated and very male.

She scanned the dresser and nightstand for any additional clues to Hank's personality, but found not one bit of evidence that would tell her his taste in books, his preference in after-shave or his family history. The room looked as though the decor had been completed by a disinterested professional the month before and as if it had been cleaned religiously each week since then. She might have attributed the tidiness to his absence had he not been in the room last night. There wasn't even a tossed-aside T-shirt or an empty beer bottle to indicate that he'd spent that time here, either. The bed had been remade with army bootcamp precision. She doubted there was even a dent in the pillow to indicate where his head had rested. No wonder the man had been appalled the first time he'd walked into her house. He was compulsively neat. Her professional training kicked in and she wondered what had caused it. The question was definitely untimely, but valid nonetheless.

A little bit stunned, she sank down on the side of the bed. "Hank?"

A worried frown creasing his brow, he knelt down in front of her and took her hands in his. "Second thoughts?"

"Not exactly. How do you live like this?" She gave an all-encompassing wave around the impersonal room.

Following the sweeping gesture, he stared around blankly. "I don't understand."

"It's so...sterile."

Shadows crossed his eyes, but he merely shrugged. "I guess I've never paid much attention to it."

"Don't you have any pictures of your parents? An ex-girlfriend? Something?"

He grinned at that. "You'd actually be happy to find a photograph of an ex-girlfriend by my bed?"

She reached out and ran her fingers through his hair, then touched his beard. "I actually think I might prefer it to this."

"Why?"

"This doesn't tell me anything about you. I feel as though I could be in the room of a complete stranger or even a totally impersonal hotel."

"You already know all you need to know about me." He drew her hand to his chest. "You know what's in here."

She shook her head. "I don't think so. How can I really know what's in your heart without understanding you? You told me about your mother and father, but there's more to growing up than that. Tell me about you, Hank. What were you like when you were a little boy? What subjects did you like in school? Did you always want to be an engineer?"

He touched a finger to her lips, then trailed it down along her jaw, finally moving to her breast, where he drew slow, deliberate circles around the already erect tip. Ann felt the effect of that lazy touch all the way down to her toes. As a distraction it was very effective, but she had no intention of letting him win out this time. In the long run, they'd both lose if she did. She seized his hand and held it, pressing her lips to the scarred knuckles.

"Talk to me," she pleaded.

"Now, Annie?" His voice was low, incredulous and threadbare with desire.

"Now," she said firmly, plumping up the pillows at the head of the bed and settling herself there. It was a deliberate attempt to put some distance between them without removing them entirely from the seductive atmosphere. This was a time-out, not an ending.

"I thought I was the one who was supposed to be on the couch for a session like this," he said with an edge in his voice.

She ignored the tone and patted the place beside her. "Join me."

He studied her intently. "You're really going to insist on this, aren't you?"

She nodded placidly, comfortable in the role of inquisitor as she hadn't been in the role of seductress. "I think I am."

He ran his fingers through his hair. She could see the debate raging inside him before he finally shrugged, kicked off his tennis shoes and settled himself beside her. "Okay, doc. It's the strangest sort of foreplay I've ever seen, but what do you want to know?'' he asked, then peered at her closely. "I hope it's not too much, because I'm not sure how long I can stand being this close to you in this bed without touching you.''

"Think of it this way,'' she said sweetly. "It'll put some of the spontaneity back into the afternoon.''

He groaned at that and tugged her down until she was lying flat beneath him, laughing. As she recognized the look in his eyes, though, the laughter suddenly died, along with her need for immediate answers. Never before had she seen such naked longing, such open loneliness and need. How was it possible that a man who'd filled his life with so many companions could seem so desperately alone? Why had he chosen her to banish the loneliness? Could she do it with her inexperienced touches? She knew only that she had to try, that she had to share with him some small measure of the joy he had brought into her life these past few weeks. If this was all they had between them, just this moment, it would be special, it would last them forever.

She smoothed the hair off his forehead. "I do want you to make love to me, Hank.'' She made the admission on a sigh. "Now.''

"Are you sure this time?''

She nodded. "Very sure. The talk can wait.''

His mouth came down on hers then, stealing the last of her declaration. The last of her doubts fled on a wave of pure sensation as his hands began to slide over her, stroking, exploring. With fingers that actually seemed to shake, he pushed her T-shirt up to expose her breasts to the tender mercies of his lips, his beard a gentle, but oh-so-seductive irritant across the sensitive flesh.

"Don't be afraid, Annie love," he whispered, when she trembled at the intensity of the feelings sweeping through her.

"This isn't something I do every day," she managed to say.

"Neither have I lately," he said with wry humor.

"But you've had so much more experience, what if..."

He touched a finger to her lips. "Annie, this is our first time together. *Ours.* No matter what's happened in the past, we've never been together like this before. I'm every bit as nervous as you are. I want it to be perfect for you and I won't know how if you won't tell me. So, you see, we're in the same boat."

Not quite, she thought as his expert touches robbed her of further arguments. Hank made love with astonishing gentleness. He taught her the way to tease and madden. His caresses were slow, provocative follow-ups to the adoration in his eyes. And, as if to prove his point that there were no comparisons being made, he told her again and again of all the things that made her special.

"I love the way your lips are a little off center," he said, his fingertip tracing the outline.

"And your hair is so soft. It's like silk," he whispered, smoothing it back, the callused pads of his fingers gently grazing her cheek in the process.

"Do you know what your eyes remind me of? The blue is usually the same shade as those fields of wildflowers in Texas, but now..." His voice dropped even lower. "Now it's like midnight."

And on it went. He made love to her from head to toe, without hesitation, without restraint, letting her see the joy she was bringing to him, commanding her with his patient, lingering touches to share it. She was practically humming from the inside out, her body quivering with excitement, covered with a light sheen of perspiration. One by one her muscles stretched taut with expectation as he played his fingers over and inside her, kissing her with increasing urgency.

"I love *you*, Annie," he whispered with added emphasis as he held himself poised above her. "Only you."

The truth of the words was in his eyes. And the ache that had been building inside her became even more compelling. "Show me," she pleaded, willing him to dispel the last of her uncertainty. "Please, Hank."

Showing her how to help, he slipped on protection. Then he entered her, so slowly that she thought she'd go mad before knowing the sensation of being filled up by him. When he was deep inside her at last, she felt complete for the very first time in her life. And as he began more of those slow, tantalizing strokes, she began to know the meaning of magic, the rhythm of fulfillment.

"You are so beautiful," he said, his voice ragged, his muscles tense with the strain of holding back.

"Please, Hank," she cried again, rising to meet his thrusts, urging him into a more frenzied pace. His musky scent lured her. The taste of his skin only teased at her hunger. She was past the need for compliments, beyond the desire for promises. She wanted release from the wild, wonderful, awful tension that had coiled so tightly inside her that she was certain she would explode with just one more gliding touch, just one more deep, demanding kiss.

Then his tongue circled the taut peak of her breast, the hot, moist stroking almost unbearably tender. The caress was gentle, incredibly gentle, but it was that which set off the flare of rockets that ripped through her, shattering the tension and carrying him along with her.

She didn't realize she'd been crying until Hank hovered over her, his expression filled with concern. He touched a finger to the tears rolling down her cheek. "Are you okay? Did I hurt you?" he murmured, his voice rough with anxiety.

"I didn't know..."

"What?" he pleaded. "Please, baby, you've got to tell me if I hurt you. I would never..."

She kissed him to stop the unnecessary apology. "No. I never knew it could be like that. It was beautiful." Her gaze swept over his face, memorizing the way it looked as he realized that he had made this first time so incredibly special for her. She'd never seen such a sense of wonder in a man's eyes before.

"Annie love, it's only going to get better. I promise you."

She ran her fingers over his chest, tangling them in the mat of wiry hairs, delighting in the freedom she suddenly felt, the awe he was beginning to instill in her. "You're always making promises to me."

"And I mean to keep every one of them."

She shook her head, clinging to one last shred of reality. "Hank, nothing is forever. We both know that better than anyone."

He rolled on his back and sighed. He took her hand and held it over his heart, which was thumping with a sure, steady, reassuring rhythm.

"I've always thought that, Annie," he confessed slowly.

Despite the fact that she'd been the one to say it, Ann realized that she'd been counting on a denial. Her heart sank when none came. His response hung heavily in the air between them, ruining their special moment.

As if he knew exactly what she was feeling, he reached over and lifted her until she was sitting astride him, her bare thighs clamped around his waist. "Now you listen to me," he said, his hands resting lightly on her hips, his gaze locked with hers. "That is what I used to believe, Annie. No more. What we have is forever. And if it takes me that long, I'm going to prove it to you."

For now, with the heat rising within her again, she needed him too much to argue. But the time would come, only too soon, when she knew she'd be proved right. Until then, though, they had this incredible magic.

The last gray streaks of twilight had turned to darkness when Hank woke her with a soft, sweet kiss.

"Time to go, sleeping beauty. If we don't pick the kids up soon, we really will have to explain our absence."

She ran her hand lovingly up his thigh, thrilling to the textures, the roughness of the hair, the warmth that cloaked solid strength. "It might be worth it."

He seized her fingers in midstroke. "Annie, you don't mean that."

"What if I do?"

He grinned and stripped away the sheet that covered her. "In that case," he murmured, rolling toward her, his hand already circling her breast.

Sensation swelled inside her at once, but practicality won out. Forcing a laugh, she rolled away. "Okay. Never mind. I think you're probably right."

"Tease," he grumbled. "Hurry up, before I change my mind and give Liz and Todd permanent custody of all those children of yours."

Still bathed in the warm afterglow of Hank's lovemaking, Ann felt contentment settle itself over her as they drove the mile or so back to Liz and Todd's. Even if this couldn't last forever, she would treasure it. She had only an instant's nervousness as they walked around the house toward the patio. They could hear the kids splashing in the pool and an occasional lazy admonition from Todd.

As they were about to turn the corner of the house, Hank stopped and drew her into his arms. "Don't forget this afternoon, Annie. Don't let it slip away."

Puzzled by the intensity in his voice, she touched his lips. "Why would you say that? Of course I won't forget."

"I saw that look in your eyes just now. I just don't want you to start analyzing it to death and come up with some crazy idea that it didn't mean anything. It was important, for both of us.''

"I know that. Really.''

He nodded finally. "Then let's go see what we've missed.''

On the patio they found Liz and Todd sprawled contentedly on chaise longues. Melissa was curled up at Liz's side, her thumb in her mouth, her blanket dragging on the red tiles.

Liz grinned up at them. "She conked out about an hour ago.''

Ann immediately felt guilty. "She wasn't upset, was she?''

"No, she was not upset,'' Liz said firmly. "Don't you dare start feeling guilty for taking a little time off. The kids hardly noticed you were gone.''

Hank groaned. "Wrong thing to say,'' he said. "Now she'll never let them out of her sight, for fear they'll forget all about her.''

"I will not,'' Ann protested, though there was this tiny twinge of guilt in the pit of her stomach that suggested there might be some truth in what he said.

"Can I get you two something to drink?'' Todd said.

Hank grinned at him. "Thought you were sleeping there for a minute, pal. Did the kids wear you out?''

"Do you have any idea how much energy is in that pool right this minute? If we could harness it, we could run a power plant,'' he said with weary admiration.

"You just stay where you are,'' Hank said sympathetically. "I'll get the drinks.''

As Hank went into the house, Ann walked over to the edge of the pool. She wasn't quite sure how she felt about the fact that the kids hadn't even seemed to notice her return, much less her absence. With the force of habit, she began counting heads.

Tracy was clinging to the wall at the deep end, kicking lazily. Paul, David and Todd's son, Kevin, were playing water polo, splashing exuberantly. Tommy was trying desperately to keep pace with them, but his movements were slightly hampered by his injured leg and by the water wings Todd had insisted he wear. Jason? She glanced around again. There was no sign of him. She turned back to Liz, an uneasy feeling stirring in the pit of her stomach.

"Liz? Where's Jason?" She forced herself to keep her voice calm.

"Isn't he in the pool?"

She shook her head as her heart began to beat wildly.

"He went into the house an hour or so ago," Todd said before panic could set in. "He's probably in Kevin's room playing video games."

The tension abated slightly, but didn't vanish. "I'll just go in and tell him we're back," she said casually, not wanting to admit her need to account for every one of her chicks.

"Ann..." Liz began, but Hank silenced her.

"Let her go, Liz. She won't be happy until she's made certain that they're all here and healthy."

She glared at him, but his remark didn't prevent her from going inside. She checked Kevin's room first. It was dark and deserted. Her panic returning, she dashed through the rest of the house, frantically flipping on lights, moving more and more quickly as she found each room empty.

"Hank," she called out finally, her voice trembling. "Oh, my God, Hank!"

He met her at the patio door. He took one look at her face and gathered her close, but not even the solid comfort he offered could counter the hysteria that seemed to be rising in her.

"What's wrong?"

She looked up into troubled eyes and felt tears welling up in her own as she clung to him. Her fingers dug into his shoulders as an awful emptiness crept through her.

"Annie?"

"I can't find him," she finally whispered in a voice filled with raw, unbearable pain. "Jason's gone."

Chapter Twelve

If anything has happened to him, I will never forgive myself," Ann said over and over as Hank led her to the kitchen table. She felt dazed and the ache that had settled in the region of her heart was worse than anything she had ever experienced. It didn't matter that Jason was sixteen and in many ways able to take care of himself. He was still just a lost and lonely kid and she'd obviously failed him. "Why didn't I see this coming?"

She looked at Hank. "It's because we . . . because I was too busy."

"No," he said adamantly. "It is not because of anything you did."

"We should have been here," she said stubbornly. "If he's hurt . . ."

"Jason is a tough kid. Nothing's going to happen to him," Hank reassured her. Ann wanted to believe him. She clung to the words like a lifeline, but these awful images kept creeping in.

"Drink this," Liz said, setting a cup of tea in front of her.

She pushed it away. "I don't want it. How can you even think about sitting around drinking tea when Jason is missing? We should be out looking for him, instead of wasting time like this," she lashed out accusingly.

She glared at all of them as they hovered over her. She blamed herself. She blamed Hank. Now she seemed to be including Liz in her anger. Listening to herself, she realized that her guilt was making her irrational, but she seemed unable to stop herself. Tears brimming over, she took a deep, calming breath and looked at Liz. "I'm sorry."

"You have nothing to be sorry for. Now, please, drink a little of the tea."

"Please, Annie," Hank said. "Listen to Liz. Todd and I will go look for Jason the minute I know you're all right."

"Of course I'm all right," she said impatiently. "It's Jason who's in trouble. We have to go after him. Three of us will be better than two. We can cover more territory."

"Sweetheart, it will be much better if you stay here. You don't know the area. Besides, it will only upset the other kids if all of us go racing off."

"Oh, my God!" she whispered. "I hadn't even thought about them. How am I going to tell them that he's gone?"

"There's no need to say anything yet," Hank said.

"But we have to. Maybe he said something to one of them about where he was going, what his plans were."

Hank shook his head. "He's too much of a loner. He wouldn't say anything. He'd just go. Now, please, Annie, just stay here with Liz and try to stay calm."

Calm? He was asking the impossible, but she finally admitted the wisdom in what he was suggesting. Someone had to stay with the kids and there really wasn't any point in upsetting them unnecessarily. But she felt so helpless and it wasn't a feeling she liked. She needed to do something. She needed to be part of the search for Jason. She needed to be there to talk to him, to find out why he'd gone, to hold him and remind him how much she cared.

As if she'd read her mind, Liz said, "Ann, he could come back here on his own. It'll be better if you're here waiting for him."

That was the most persuasive argument of all. Giving in finally, she sighed and buried her face in her hands.

Hank hunkered down beside her chair and took her hands and folded them tightly in his. She couldn't bring herself to meet his gaze, though.

"I'll find him, Annie," he said. "I promise."

Yet another promise. She heard the conviction in his voice, but she heard something else as well: fear. Was he more afraid for Jason than he'd admitted or was he afraid of what this would do to the two of them? Perhaps both. God knows that's how she felt. She was torn apart inside thinking about what could be happening to Jason. She also knew that things might never be the same between her and Hank if their time together had been the cause of his running away. Blame and guilt would always be there between them, eating away at the fiber of their still-new relationship.

When Hank and Todd had left, she looked over at Liz and finally dared to speak her fears aloud. "It's my fault. I never should have left here this afternoon. I knew how much he resented Hank and I went off with him anyway."

"Don't be ridiculous. You have every right to a life of your own, Ann. You owe it to yourself to grab for whatever happiness you can find. You're long overdue."

"Not at the expense of my children."

"Spending one afternoon with Hank is not robbing your children of anything and, as much as you love them, they do not have the right to choose your friends or your lovers."

How many times had she counseled divorced parents on just that point? Living through it for the first time herself, she began to fully understand the complexities, the mine field of explosive emotions involved. Nothing was as clear-cut and easy as she'd always made it sound. "But they weren't prepared," she told Liz. "We should have talked about it."

"Do you honestly expect me to believe that you were going to sit those kids down and tell them that you wanted to go off to make love with Hank?"

Ann felt the color rise in her cheeks. "Well, I certainly wouldn't have put it like that. I could have told them that we were going out, though, instead of just sneaking away like a couple of teenagers trying to escape the watchful eyes of their parents."

Liz sighed. "Okay. I can't deny that that might have been the wise thing to do, but not doing it is hardly the end of the world. You did not behave irresponsibly. You didn't leave them alone. They were here with us. They were having a good time. There are five kids out on the patio who did not suffer any emotional harm just because you needed some time to yourself."

"But there's one who did."

"You have to stop thinking that way. You don't know that Jason's leaving had anything to do with that. He's been troubled since the day he moved in with you. Maybe he just picked today to take off because he thought he could get away with it."

When Ann started to deny Jason's ongoing behavior problems, Liz held up her hand. "Don't forget how many conversations you and I have had on just that subject."

Ann felt her shoulders sag. It was true. She had admitted more than once to Liz things she'd refused to acknowledge to Hank. It was as if she'd wanted Hank's approval of Jason so much that she'd been afraid to acknowledge to him that the boy had problems that needed correcting, problems that she'd found herself unable to address.

"For a psychologist, I've really mucked this one up royally, haven't I?"

"That's because you're a mother first and mothers sometimes make mistakes. We're not nearly as dispassionate and objective when one of our own's involved. You've spent so much time worrying about Jason's terrible past that you haven't been nearly as tough as you should have been in guiding his present. That's a very human reaction."

Seized by sudden uncertainty, Ann asked, "Do you think I can make it up to him?"

"I'm not sure you have anything to make up to Jason, if that's what you're asking. You've given that boy every chance. You've loved him as if he were your own. He's repaid you with nothing but heartache."

Ann smiled ruefully. "Actually, I wasn't talking just about Jason. I was thinking of Hank, too. I was awfully hard on him."

Liz grinned back at her. "Oh, I'm sure you can make it up to him. Hank's got a tough hide, but he's a real softie inside. I found that out when he had a heart-to-heart talk with me when I was about to walk out of Todd's life. Just make sure you tell him that you don't blame him for any of this. After all, Todd and I are the ones who let Jason get away."

"But I don't blame any of you, not really."

"I know. You only blame yourself, but there was a minute there, before Hank walked out the door, when I think everyone in this room got the idea that you did blame him."

"I'll talk to him," she vowed. "As soon as Jason is back safely..."

Left unsaid was what she would do if they didn't find Jason. Ann refused to let herself even consider the possibility. They had to find him. They had to. Her entire future with Hank might very well depend on it.

Hank had no idea how good Jason's sense of direction might be, but he was relatively certain the boy would try to make his way back to the highway so he could get back to the Keys. In fact, if he had enough of a head start, he suspected Jason would go straight to Key West. Back home. Even though it had never been much of a home to him, Key West was the one place Jason ever spoke of with genuine enthusiasm. Hank only prayed he could find him before Jason hitched a ride. Despite his reassurances for Ann's benefit, he didn't like the idea of what could happen to a kid hitchhiking.

As he drove up and down the dark, winding streets, he cursed himself for not anticipating something like this. He was the one who'd recognized Jason's increasing alienation, his obvious resentment of the place Hank was filling in Ann's life. He should have talked to the boy, instead of losing patience with his surliness. If nothing else, he'd owed it to Ann to try harder. He was the grown-up, not Jason. Maybe he wasn't father material after all. Just when he'd begun to think he had it in him to deal with family life, something like this happened to prove that he was a pretender.

His spirits sank lower and lower. By the time he finally spotted Jason walking along the side of a narrow road, half-hidden in the shadows, he was nearly out of his mind with worry and self-condemnation. Where was the kid's head, he thought furiously when he could barely pick him out alongside the darkened roadway. Wearing blue jeans and a navy-blue polo shirt while walking at night was a good way to get hit by a passing car.

Before he could make the mistake of yelling, though, he warned himself to slow down. Getting into an absurd argument over where Jason had chosen to walk and the clothes he was wearing wouldn't help anything.

"Jason," he called out, keeping his tone carefully neutral. "Hop in."

Jason kept his gaze straight ahead. His pace never faltered.

"Son," he began, only to have Jason whirl around, his expression furious.

"You are not my father!" he shouted, then took off, nearly tripping and falling in his haste to get away.

Taken aback by the anger and raw emotion, Hank stared after him for an instant before driving slowly up beside him again. "You're right," he called out. "I'm not your father. I'm sorry."

In the blue-white glow of the headlights, he could detect the sheen of tears on Jason's cheeks and suddenly his heart turned over. For the first time he truly recognized the scared, vulnerable boy inside that tough facade. With that recognition came another blow: the person Jason most reminded him of in this world was himself some twenty years ago. He didn't like the fact that he hadn't admitted it sooner.

"Jason, let's go somewhere and talk about this," he suggested quietly, determined to find a way to make things right between them. This time it was not just for Ann's sake, but for his own.

"I got nothing to say to you."

"And what about Ann? Do you have any idea how scared she is right now?"

Jason's step faltered.

"She's back at Liz and Todd's blaming herself because you left. She thinks she failed you."

"She didn't do nothing," Jason mumbled.

"You and I both know that, but she doesn't. All she knows is that you've gone and she's convinced if she'd been there, she could have stopped you. But this is between you and me, isn't it?"

That drew Jason's gaze to him. The stark honesty of the words created a palpable tension between them and something new, Hank thought. Hope.

"Isn't it?" he persisted.

"Maybe."

"Then let's go get a soda or something and talk about it, man-to-man."

"Since when?" Jason said sarcastically. "You always treat me like some dumb kid. Until you came along, Ann always treated me like a grown-up. She depended on me."

And that, of course, was a large part of the problem that he'd never before recognized. Why hadn't he seen it before? As Jason saw it, his role in Ann's life had been usurped by a stranger. Hank had to prove to him that they both belonged, that she had more than enough love for the two of them.

"Fair enough," he said. "That's something we should talk about."

Hank thought he caught a flicker of hope in Jason's eyes before his shoulders sagged. "What's the point?" he muttered, starting to walk again.

"The point is that we both love Ann. Neither of us wants her to be unhappy, so we owe it to her to try to work out our differences," he said firmly. "Don't we?"

Jason hesitated.

"Jason? Don't we?"

"I guess," he said with obvious reluctance.

"Will you get in, then?"

Jason finally turned grudgingly and opened the door. He got into the car, but he huddled as close to the door as he could get. Hank drove to a fast-food restaurant a few blocks away and led him inside.

"Hungry?"

"I guess."

"Well, I'm starved. How about a burger, fries, something to drink?"

Jason shrugged. Hank placed the order, then carried it to a booth. When Jason had wolfed down his sandwich and the french fries, Hank asked him quietly, "Okay, why don't you tell me why you ran away?"

"What do you care, man? I'm just in your way. You were probably glad I was gone."

"Then why am I here?"

"Because Ann sent you."

Hank shook his head. "No, it's more than that. I never wanted you to leave, Jason. I wouldn't put Ann through this kind of pain for anything in the world. Don't you realize how very important you are to Ann?

I love her, so I wanted to be a father to you, but I didn't know how. Did you ever stop to think that maybe I'm just as much afraid as you are?''

"Afraid? Right," Jason scoffed, but Hank could tell that the idea intrigued him.

"It's true. You know, I never had much of a family life myself. My dad left before I was born and my mom, well, she wasn't around a whole lot. I got pretty used to being on my own. I didn't have any brothers or sisters, so I had no idea what family life was like. Todd was the best friend I had and his family wasn't too great, either, so I've always been real careful not to get too involved with anyone. I figured that was just asking for trouble. Know what I mean?''

Jason's brown eyes were watching him with avid interest now. He nodded slowly.

"When I came to stay with Ann in the Keys, I didn't expect to like it there. It was a place to stay, that's all. I'd only met Ann once and, to tell you the truth, we hadn't gotten along all that well. As for you guys, well, the idea of a bunch of kids scared the daylights out of me. What did I know about kids? Not much. Then I started getting to know you all. Tracy and the others, they made it easy, but not you. You were just the way I was when I was your age. You'd built this wall around you and I didn't know how to get past it. Maybe that's why I've been so hard on you. Nobody made it easy for me. Nobody loved me the way Ann loves you. I figured you ought to learn to appreciate what you had. I thought maybe that job would teach you something about responsibility, about pulling your own weight.''

"I just thought you wanted me out of the way," Jason finally admitted. "I figured the minute I was making some money, you'd be trying to talk me into leaving."

"Hey, I may make mistakes, some of them pretty good-size ones, but I'm not dumb. Do you know what Ann would do to me if I tried to get you out of that house?"

Jason grinned suddenly. "You mean after she chased you around with a butcher knife?"

Hank grinned back. "Yeah, after that."

"Maybe tar and feathers."

The idea seemed to appeal to him a lot. Hank tried not to wince at the enthusiasm. "Oh, I think she'd probably think even that was too good for me. She loves all you kids and she'd do anything in the world to protect you."

Jason's expression suddenly became troubled. His voice dropped to a nervous whisper. "How mad do you think she's gonna be that I ran away?"

"Oh, I think a month in your room ought to about cover it," Hank said lightly.

Jason squirmed. "I guess that's better than being tarred and feathered."

"Considerably," Hank concurred. "Ready to go back?"

"Can I ask you something else?"

Hank nodded.

"Are you and Ann gonna get married, like Tracy said?"

"If I have my way, we are. How would you feel about that?"

"It's not up to me."

"That's where you're wrong. What you think is very important to her. She'll never do anything if she thinks it would truly hurt one of you."

Jason's expression suddenly grew cocky. "So it's sort of like you need my permission, huh?"

Hank had to choke back a laugh. "Sort of."

"I guess that sort of changes things, doesn't it?"

He stood and ruffled Jason's hair. "Not that much, kid. Not that much."

Jason looked increasingly uneasy as they drew closer to Liz and Todd's. "Maybe we could just tell her that I went for a walk," he suggested hopefully.

Hank returned his look seriously. "But that would be a lie."

"So, big deal. She wouldn't worry so much, then."

"She wouldn't have worried if you'd told her that *before* you ran away. Since you didn't, the worrying is already done."

"Yeah, I guess. It was worth a shot, though."

Jason's footsteps began to lag behind as they approached the house, but Hank was already calling out. Ann came racing through the living room, Liz just a few steps behind her. Ann's expression went from stark terror to relief and then delight in a matter of seconds. Since Jason was standing perfectly still just inside the front door, she came to him and took him in her arms.

"You cost me ten years off my life," she said in a voice that was thick with emotion.

"I'm sorry," Jason said, his skinny arms going awkwardly around her.

She looked from Jason to Hank and back again. "Is everything okay?"

Hank nodded. "I think everything is going to be just fine."

She cupped Jason's face in her hands and scanned his expression closely. "What about you? What do you think?"

Hank felt his breath catch in his chest as he waited for Jason's reply. He had a feeling his future and not just Jason's hung in the balance.

"I guess it'll be okay."

Ann wrapped the embarrassed boy in another tight hug. She looked at Hank over Jason's head.

Thank you, she mouthed silently.

He nodded.

Everything was going to be just fine, he told himself repeatedly over the next few days, but it was hard to believe it. Ann never let any of the kids out of her sight for long. She also did everything she could to avoid being alone with Hank. She'd even stopped running, claiming that she had to catch up on paperwork in the mornings. They'd been back in the Keys for nearly a week before he finally called her on it.

"Okay, Annie, why are you avoiding me?" he said, lingering after the last of the kids had left the kitchen.

"I'm not avoiding you."

"No? How would I get a crazy idea like that, then?"

"Your imagination?" she suggested, inching toward the door.

He shook his head. "Nope. I think it has more to do with the fact that you have not been in a room alone with me since last Saturday afternoon."

"We're alone now."

"For how long? You have one foot out the door. The only thing that's kept you here is that you're too polite to walk out on me in midsentence."

Flustered, Ann returned his challenging gaze. He was right. She had been avoiding him. When they'd come back on Saturday night to find that Jason had taken off, she had realized anew that there were too many things standing in the way of their making any sort of future plans. She owed him an apology for blaming him for Jason's running away, but beyond that they needed to keep their distance. They certainly couldn't have a wild affair with six children in the house. And they couldn't very well go sneaking around. Just look what had happened the first time they'd tried that.

So she'd made up her mind to think of Saturday as a wonderful interlude. It had proved to her that she could still feel, that she was a woman with a passionate nature and emotions that ran deep. Think of it as a test, she told herself. She had passed.

Now what?

Now she had to get out of this kitchen before Hank kissed her, which was what it looked as though he had every intention of doing. She scooted through the door. He was faster. He had one hand locked around her wrist before she could make the turn into the first hallway.

"Running, Annie?"

"I . . . I thought I heard one of the kids," she said nervously as her pulse leaped wildly. His mouth hovered near hers, taunting her with the reminder of its velvet softness, its moist heat, its hungry demands.

"I didn't hear a thing, except for the sound of your heart beating."

She backed up a step. The wall stopped her. She pressed hard against it anyway, as if hoping it would yield to her desire to flee. "Hank, why are you pushing this? You don't really want a relationship with me."

He stared back at her. "I don't?"

Admittedly, he did look incredulous, but she said firmly, "You don't. It's just an infatuation, a passing fancy. You know."

He pulled her tight against him. His body was solid and hard and every bit as unyielding as that wall. He smelled of the slightly spicy scent of his soap. "What I know is," he began, his breath whispering across her cheek, "you are the only thing in this life that I do want. I thought I proved that to you on Saturday."

"No," she said, ducking out of the circle of his arms. "All that proved was that there is some undeniable chemistry between us. If we ignore it, it will go away."

He brought her right back against him, where it was very clear that the chemistry was hard at work again. Her heart skittered wildly, then settled into a galloping rhythm that proved her point. Chemistry. That's all it was.

"This is not some high-school science experiment," he murmured. "I am not trying to prove some theory about opposites attracting or what happens when two incendiary devices collide in the night."

She cleared her throat. "What . . . what are you trying to prove?"

"That you can tell yourself from now until those dolphins of yours learn to speak fluent Italian, German and Spanish that this is nothing but a passing fancy, but I will be right here, in this house, in your bed, proving you wrong."

She shook her head, but it didn't seem to carry much conviction. She wanted to believe that fierce look of possessiveness in his eyes. She wanted to believe in the wonder of his touch. She wanted to believe so badly, she ached with it, but she wouldn't let him know that.

"Accept it, Annie," he said. His lips against her throat gave heated emphasis to the demand.

She swallowed back a gasp of pleasure and tried to rally indignation. "In your dreams," she said boldly.

He grinned, blast him all to hell and back.

"That's right," he said sweetly. "In my dreams."

And, then, with a final kiss that stole the last of her breath away, he left her to her dreams. She didn't need a textbook to figure out what they meant. The tangled sheets and aching need swelling low in her belly told her all she needed to know.

Chapter Thirteen

Ann badly needed to run. Maybe if she ran far enough and fast enough, she could reduce the stressful effect of Hank's nonstop flirting. Her nerves were so ragged she could barely get through the day without wanting to scream.

Finally, in an act of sheer desperation, she set her alarm a half hour earlier than usual. Maybe she could sneak out of the house before he got up and put in five miles of hard running before breakfast. She spent most of the night rolling over and checking the clock, just to be sure she wouldn't sleep through the alarm. Ten minutes before it was due to go off, she hit the switch and dragged herself out of bed. She tugged on her clothes in record time, ran her fingers hastily through her hair and tiptoed through the still-dark house. She went straight through the kitchen, not even pausing to put on the coffee pot or do her warm-ups. She'd do the exercises outside, where there was less chance of Hank hearing her.

She had put one foot on the porch when she heard the creak of a rocking chair, and Hank's quiet, "Morning, Annie."

It was all she could do to keep from crying in frustration. "Why are you up?" she asked, unable to keep the annoyance from her voice.

"Waiting for you."

"But I didn't . . . I'm not usually . . ." She glared at him. "How did you know?"

"Calculated guess. Besides, I've heard you tossing and turning for the past week. I figured sooner or later you'd have to get back into your routine and work off your frustrations."

"Frustrations?" she said weakly.

He chuckled. "You know about frustration, Annie. It's what happens when a person tries to deny their feelings, especially their sexual feelings."

She could feel heat flooding her cheeks. "I am not denying my feelings."

"Then why can't you sleep?"

"I . . . I have a lot on my mind."

"Me?"

"Don't flatter yourself. Now leave me alone. I'm going running."

"Stretch first," he warned.

She had absolutely no intention of standing in front of Hank Riley and stretching while he ogled her. She took off across the yard, walking briskly. Hank strolled after her. She broke into a trot. Hank loped along beside her. She increased her pace. With a barely perceptible output of effort, Hank kept in step.

This was not reducing her stress. This was driving her crazy.

"Hank, why are you doing this?" she asked plaintively.

"Doing what?"

"Pestering me."

"Is that what I'm doing? I thought I was keeping you company."

"I don't want company."

"You will when your muscles knot up because you didn't warm up."

"My muscles will be just fine," she said. But with a perversity she should have expected, her calf tensed painfully. She winced and tried to run through the pain. It got worse, until she was finally forced to slow down. Naturally Hank was gloating.

"Give me your leg."

"There is nothing wrong with my leg."

"Oh, for heaven's sakes, woman, sit down and let me massage your leg."

It hurt too badly to refuse. She limped over to a tree stump and sat down. Hank knelt in front of her. But the minute his strong fingers curved around her calf, every other muscle in her body tensed.

"Relax, Annie. This is not a seduction."

The reassurance was not convincing. It felt like a seduction. Only the setting seemed incongruous. With sure strokes, Hank continued to knead her leg. The muscle finally loosened. The pain eased.

"I'm okay now," she said shakily.

"As long as I'm down here, there's something I want to ask you."

She regarded him warily. "What?"

"Marry me, Annie."

Every muscle froze again. Hank unconsciously began massaging. "Well?" he said.

Her throat was so dry she couldn't squeak out a single word. Nervously she licked her lips. "That sounds more like an order than a question," she evaded.

His lips twitched. "Okay. I'll try again. Will you marry me?"

"Why?"

His fingers were sliding up and down her leg, creating more of that unbearable tension that curled low in her abdomen. "Because I love you."

The words hovered between them, the most powerful temptation on the face of the earth, next to the effect of his touch.

"Hank, face it," she said, trying desperately to cling to rational thought when she was oh-so-tempted to throw herself straight into his arms. "You and I would drive each other crazy inside of a month."

"Probably less," he concurred. "That doesn't mean it's not worth a try."

"*A try?* That's your idea of marriage?"

"Annie, I am not good with words. You know what I mean. What we have is special. It's something I never experienced growing up. I never had a father. I had a mother who didn't know the meaning of love. Now that I finally understand what it is, I don't want to let it slip away."

"Hank, you don't understand anything about love. What you're feeling is the challenge, the excitement of the chase. Once you've conquered all my reservations, once you've gotten me in front of a preacher to say all those pretty words about love and honor, it would lose its excitement. You'd be bored."

"In this household I'd have to be dead to be bored. There hasn't been a dull moment since the day I moved in."

He sounded so convincing. The look in his eyes practically scorched her with its intensity. But she knew better. He'd only been there a couple of months. The novelty hadn't worn off yet. But it would and she would not put them both through the torment of a divorce when that happened.

"No, Hank. And if you bring it up again, I'll send you packing."

If he was disappointed, he didn't show it. He simply held out his hand and helped her to her feet. "Let's go, Annie."

She was suddenly feeling oddly let down. Finishing the run would fix that, she told herself briskly, and began jogging.

"Annie?" Hank said beside her. She glanced over at him. "You can't possibly run fast enough to get away from me."

There was a deliberate taunt in his voice when he said it, but it was the glint of determination in his eyes that set her blood on fire.

Whispers. Ann had never before noticed so much whispering going on around the house. Usually she felt like wearing earmuffs to shut out the yelling. Now, though, every time she walked into a room she was greeted by sudden silence and guilty looks. They were in cahoots all right, but why? If her birthday hadn't been months away, she'd have thought they were planning a surprise party.

Whatever was going on, Hank didn't seem to be in on it. She'd noticed that the kids were being just as secretive around him. It was beginning to get on her nerves, which were already shaky enough thanks to Hank's lingering looks and deliberately casual touches. She continued to try to avoid him, but that wasn't working one bit better than solving the mystery of the children's behavior.

She was sitting with him in the kitchen late one night, unable to think of a thing to say to combat the increasingly tense silence, when she finally said in desperation, "Have you noticed that the kids are being a little weird these days?"

"Weird?" He shook his head. "How?"

"Quiet. Secretive. What do you suppose they're up to?"

"Maybe they're planning an overthrow of the household leadership," he joked.

She scowled impatiently. "Very funny. I'm trying to be serious here. All the sneaking around has me worried."

"Forget it, Annie. Do you see any evidence that they're upset about anything?"

"No," she admitted.

"Even Jason has been on his best behavior since the trip to Miami, right?"

"I suppose so."

"And Tracy's not as moody."

"True." Tracy had, however, started offering to lend her clothes in colors she knew Hank liked. She'd even brought home a new blusher, eye shadow and a bolder shade of lipstick and left them openly on Ann's dresser. The hints were obvious and, no doubt, part of the whole plot that had her worried.

"But don't you think it's odd . . ." she began.

"Ann, there is nothing to worry about. Drink your tea."

He was trying to placate her. She recognized the tone. It added to her jittery state of mind. "It's so pleasant to have someone to talk things over with," she snapped irritably.

"I'm glad you feel that way," he said, deliberately misinterpreting her sarcasm. "There's something I've been meaning to talk to you about."

"Well, you can just go to hell. I have nothing to say to you."

She got up and stomped out of the room, passing Tracy and Jason in the doorway. She caught the odd look that passed between them, but she was too furious to try to interpret it. Right now all she wanted to do was get away from Hank and the emotions that seemed to get all tangled up inside her whenever she was in his presence.

She had wasted an entire afternoon in her office stretched out on her sofa trying to analyze what was happening between them. She'd viewed it as something of a private therapy session. She had toted up Hank's attributes, which were many. She had pinpointed each and every one of his flaws, also legion, and decided, on balance, that there was no rational reason to consider a future with the man. He would never be the placid, rock-solid, even-tempered man she'd always dreamed of sharing her life with. He was volatile and unpredictable on the one hand and too darned neat on the other. Even if she could get those awful doughnuts from him, she'd probably never get him to give up the rest of his junk food.

Stop being petty, some little voice had nagged. None of that really matters. What mattered was the fact that she knew deep down inside that Hank didn't really want to be a family man. He was kind and generous, the kind of man who'd even give a meal to a stray cat, but that didn't mean he'd keep it around for the rest of his life. He didn't want that sort of long-term commitment. He'd practically told her as much when he'd revealed the secrets of his childhood. Forget all her degrees, even an amateur psychologist could figure out the impact his mother's behavior had had on his ability to relate to women. She understood all that. She really did. Better, apparently, than he did himself.

So, she had concluded at the end of the session, she was just going to treat him casually for the few remaining weeks they were likely to have together. They would part as friends. Good friends. Caring friends.

Not lovers.

"You know, Annie," said the voice of her good, caring friend right behind her. A shiver shot down her spine and made mincemeat of her intentions.

She whipped around angrily. "Stop doing that!"

"Doing what?"

"Sneaking up on me."

"I did not sneak up on you," he said reasonably. "I walked out of the kitchen right behind you. I did nothing to hide my actions. You were just lost in thought. What were you thinking about, Annie?"

She recognized that innocently quizzical expression in his eyes. More important, she spotted the neatly set trap. He wasn't catching her in it. No, sir. "Nothing in particular," she said in a voice so cool it could have chilled champagne. "Was there something you wanted?"

Blue eyes lost their innocence at once. They captured her and pinned her right where she was with masculine intensity. Her heart skittered crazily.

"Hank," she protested weakly.

"Hmm?"

"I asked if there was something you wanted."

"Yes," he murmured, leaning toward her, his gaze fastened on her mouth.

"I meant something else," she said. Her voice sounded strangled.

"First things first."

She took a hastily drawn and very deep breath, then darted past him calling at the top of her lungs, "Melissa! Time for bed."

She heard him sigh heavily as she made her narrowest escape yet. And for just a minute, she felt a fleeting pang of regret. Then she reminded herself that what she was doing was in her own best interests and in Hank's. It was getting harder and harder to remember that, though.

Hank retreated to the backyard hammock. It was getting to be absurd. He was acting like a third grader with a crush trying to steal kisses on a playground from a reluctant classmate. That's what Ann had reduced him to with her stubborn denial that anything had changed between them on the trip to Miami. Whether she would have behaved exactly the same way had Jason not run away was a moot point. The fact remained that she was intentionally distancing herself from him. And he, despite his reputation as a ladies' man, had no idea what to do about it. He'd thought the marriage proposal would convince her, but it had only made her more skittish than ever. It left him completely at a loss.

Ann was not one bit like the women he'd been attracted to in the past. A dozen roses, a bottle of expensive wine or a box of imported chocolates would be wasted on her. She had a yard filled with rose bushes, she wasn't crazy about wine and he could just imagine what she'd have to say about the candy. He could always send her a gallon jug of apple juice or bring her a dozen oat-bran muffins, but where was the romance in that? As for taking her out to a candlelit dinner, she'd probably insist on hauling all six children along. They'd wind up taking a vote and eating pizza. It was hard to be seductive over tomato sauce. He couldn't even impress her by taking her to the ballet or the symphony. The nearest performances were in Miami and she'd never even consider going with him and staying overnight, not after what had happened last time.

He knew, despite her denials, that she was every bit as attracted to him as he was to her. In fact, if he had to put a label on what they were both feeling, he would call it love. He was the first to admit he hadn't had all that much experience with the emotion. On those rare occasions when he'd even allowed himself to believe in its existence, he'd imagined it to be more pleasurable than this, more carefree. Instead it seemed to be made up of giddy highs and astonishingly painful lows. And, in their case, instead of a simple, joyous union between two consenting adults, it seemed to involve a package deal that brought out protective instincts so deep he was shaken by them.

He wanted not just Ann's happiness, but Jason's and Tracy's and Paul's and David's and Tommy's and Melissa's. When any one of them hurt, he hurt. He knew Ann felt the same way...about the six children. Her devotion to them was unquestioning and freely given. He was the only person she didn't trust enough to allow herself to love without hesitation. She was still terrified that he would walk out on them, leaving the kids shaken and her heart in tatters.

Their relationship needed time. He had to prove to her that he wasn't going anywhere, that his wandering days were long past. The only way to do that was to stick around. Unfortunately, his role in the Marathon project was nearing completion. In another month or so he'd be able to move back to Miami and make only occasional site visits. Unless he could dream up an excuse to stay, he was out of here by early April at the latest.

He was still trying to think of a solution to his dilemma when Tracy came out of the house.

"Hank?" she called hesitantly.

"Over here."

She walked over and settled down cross-legged on the ground beside the hammock.

"What's up?" he asked when she didn't say anything.

"Do you think it would be okay if I borrowed the car tomorrow night?"

"I'm not the person you should be asking."

"I can't ask Ann."

"Why not? She's always let you use her car before. Are you planning to go someplace she wouldn't approve of?"

"Not exactly."

"That's not an explanation."

"I know."

"And you're not going to say any more?"

He could see her shake her head. "Then I guess you're going to have to forget about the car."

"How about your truck? Could I use that?"

"Not without an explanation."

"Don't you trust me?"

Hoping she couldn't see the grin in the nighttime shadows, he said, "Not fair, young lady."

"But if you really trusted me, you'd take my word that this is really, really important and you wouldn't ask any questions."

"If you were twenty-two, I might agree, but you are barely eighteen."

"So I can't take the truck, either?"

Hank sat up in the hammock and turned until he could get a good look at Tracy's face. "Why is this so important? Can't you tell me that?"

"No. It would ruin everything."

"Ruin what?"

She jumped to her feet. "Oh, never mind. I'll think of something else."

She started across the lawn, her shoulders slumped dejectedly. Hank debated for several seconds. He knew Tracy was a good driver and she was a responsible girl.

"Tracy."

She stopped and waited.

"You can borrow the truck."

She ran back and threw her arms around him. "Thanks, Hank. You won't be sorry. I promise I'll be really, really careful."

He tilted her chin up. "You'd better be or Ann will kill both of us."

Tracy picked the truck up at the construction site the next afternoon at three. Hank got a ride home with his foreman a couple of hours later. As he walked into the kitchen, he took one look around and came to a speechless halt.

The table was covered with a white damask cloth. Two candles had been placed in the center, along with a huge bowl of pink roses. The scent filled the room. Two places had been set with the good china, the silver and the crystal. For once, in fact, everything matched. Jason's stereo cassette player was sitting on the kitchen counter with a selection of tapes stacked in front of it. Hank scanned the labels and grinned.

Someone had very romantic taste and he had a suspicion who it was. Tracy. She had plotted this. That's what all the secrecy had been about. And she had borrowed the truck to take the kids away for the evening, so he and Ann could be alone.

A setup like this called for a spectacular meal. Tracy, however, was a little shaky when it came to cooking. He could hardly wait to see what she'd left in the oven. He opened the door, leaned down and peered in. Some sort of chicken dish was simmering at the low temperature. It smelled and looked superb. Startled, he stood and looked around, chuckling when he saw the empty boxes from a gourmet grocery store. In front of the microwave he found vegetables and rice, and in the refrigerator there were bowls heaped with strawberries beside a pitcher of cream. Instead of wine, there was a chilled bottle of sparkling cider. It appeared they'd thought of everything. All this effort removed any uncertainty he might have had about how the kids would feel about a closer, more permanent involvement between him and Ann.

If they'd gone to this much trouble, the least he could do was cooperate. He took a hurried shower, found a pair of decent slacks among the jeans he'd brought with him and a pinstriped shirt. He looked at the sports jacket hanging in the closet and shrugged. What the hell! He might as well go all out. Annie had never seen him dressed in anything more formal than jeans. Not since Liz and Todd's wedding, anyway. It hadn't made much of an impression on her then, but maybe now it would be just the thing to throw her off balance and into his arms.

When he was ready, he went back to the kitchen, popped one of the tapes into the player, lit the candles, dimmed the lights and poured himself a glass of cider. Then he settled back to wait. As the minutes ticked by, his nerves stretched so taut he was afraid they'd snap. It was after six when he finally heard her car pull into the driveway. Feeling like a teenager on prom night, he stood and faced the door.

Ann stepped through the door and without even looking around, flipped on the lights. Hank took one look at her expression and his spirits fell. She didn't seem surprised. She didn't seem pleased. She looked as though someone had dealt a blow to her midsection from which she was still reeling.

"Annie," he said softly, taking a tentative step toward her. She looked toward him, her eyes finally focusing on his face. There was so much hurt there. Her cheeks were streaked with tears. "Annie love, what's happened? Are you okay?"

He folded his arms around her and felt a shudder sweep through her. "Please, sweetheart, you're scaring me. What's wrong?"

Her arms crept around his waist and she clung to him, sobbing as though her heart had broken. Hank felt something tear loose inside him as he held her. "It's okay," he murmured, rubbing his hands up and down her back as if to ward off a chill. "Shh. It's okay."

"No," she said, her voice ragged from all the tears she'd shed.

"Then tell me. Let me help."

"It's Melissa."

Hank's heart began to hammer harder. Melissa, dear God, if anything had happened to their baby, if Tracy had had an accident . . .

"What . . ." he began and realized that his own throat was so thick with emotion he could barely speak.

"They called."

"Who called?" he demanded, his fingers digging into her arms. "Dammit, Ann, is she hurt? What?"

"They want to take her away from me."

Chapter Fourteen

Take her away?'' Hank repeated in a daze. There was a huge knot in the pit of his stomach. He kept remembering the warm, tender feelings that crept over him whenever Melissa held out her chubby little arms for a hug, whenever she stared at him with those huge, innocent blue eyes. The unexpected power of those emotions had held him captive for weeks now.

''What does that mean?'' he asked, studying the agonized expression in Ann's eyes and feeling his own chest constrict in pain. ''Can they do that? Can they just come in here and take her?''

''They can do whatever they want,'' Ann said wearily. ''She's a ward of the state. I'm just her foster mother.''

''But why would they take her away? Can't they see how traumatic it would be for a three-year-old to be uprooted again? Explain it to them. You're more than just a foster mother. You're a psychologist. Surely they'll listen."

"It's not that simple. The mother has finally relinquished custody, which makes Melissa eligible for adoption." Ann's bleak, uncommonly submissive tone only heightened his dismay. Her eyes were luminous with tears. "There's this couple, Hank. They want her." Though she was trying to sound so brave, her voice broke, carving a jagged path through his heart. "They want to adopt my baby and the state thinks it would be best for Melissa to have two parents. How can I argue?"

Hank tried to gather his composure, when what he felt like doing was bashing his fist into a wall or better yet into the face of whatever bureaucrat was making this heartless decision. Couldn't they see that no one would ever be a better parent to Melissa than Annie?

Right now, though, her vulnerability left him shaken. She needed him to be strong. She needed him to cling to for once. Now was no time for him to be falling apart or charging out of here and doing something rash. They needed to do some clear thinking. He didn't know the ins and outs of state regulations, but surely there was a way to block this. Melissa was theirs. She loved them. They loved her. It was as simple—and as complex, apparently—as that.

"We'll fight it," he said flatly. "There must be things we can do. We'll apply to adopt her ourselves. Sit down, I'll make you some tea and we can talk about it."

Obviously drained, Ann sank down in a chair, folded her arms on the table and lowered her head. His thoughts reeling, Hank put the teakettle on the stove and tried to calm down. His outrage at the injustice of this wouldn't help now. He poured the tea finally and put the cup in front of her. "Drink it, Annie. It'll make you feel better."

She lifted her head and managed a trembling grin. "Don't tell me now you've finally become a convert."

"To what?" he said, staring at her blankly as he sank down in a chair across from her.

"Tea."

"Annie, I don't care what you drink. Personally, I could use a stiff shot of Scotch. The point is we have to make some decisions and I gather we don't have a lot of time."

She shook her head wearily. "Not we, Hank. Me. I have to make the decisions. I appreciate your concern, but it's my problem."

His heart hammering, Hank stood so fast his chair went spinning. It crashed into the counter. "Dammit, Annie, this isn't just some friendly concern on my part. Don't you think this matters to me, too? That little girl is mine just as much as if I'd fathered her." He slammed the chair back against the table and leaned down until he was mere inches from her. She swallowed convulsively as he said with slow, furious emphasis, "I have tucked her into bed. I have read her stories. I've bandaged her cuts and kissed away her tears. Dammit, Annie, I love her, too!" He fought to hold back tears of rage and frustration.

Looking stunned by his tirade, Ann simply stared at him. "You love her," she whispered wonderingly, touching a finger to his cheek. Her voice shook.

He hunkered down beside her and clasped her hands. "Of course I love her. What did you think?"

"I don't know. I guess I thought you'd just gotten used to her, to all of us."

"Annie, I love every crazy, troublesome, charming, infuriating person in this house and that includes you," he said fervently, cupping her chin in his hand. "If I had my way, we'd be married by tomorrow morning and we'd adopt every one of those kids and maybe even add a couple more of our own."

"But you . . . you've always been so . . ." She threw up her hands. "You know, so single."

He grinned. "So alone. That's what I've been, Annie. I've been on my own emotionally for so many years that I didn't know what it could be like to have other people in my life, to share good times and bad times, to have someone waiting for me at the end of the day. I was scared to death to enjoy it, because I was so afraid that by morning it could all be gone. I've finally accepted the fact that real love doesn't go away. It doesn't vanish in a puff of smoke. Sometimes you might have to work a little to hang on to it and it's not always magic and rainbows, but it's the best thing we're ever likely to have going for us. The tough times make the magic even more special and the rainbows even brighter."

Ann's smile trembled tentatively on her lips before finally turning bright. She curved her hand over his and held it against her cheek. Tears slid down, pooling against their clasped fingers. "You can be downright eloquent when you try, Hank Riley."

He drew her palm to his lips and kissed it. "As long as I seem to be getting through to you at last, did I mention again that I want to marry you?"

"You mentioned it, but once again you didn't ask."

"Then let me correct that at once. Will you marry me, Annie?" He gestured around the kitchen. "The kids went to all this trouble to set the scene. We wouldn't want to waste it."

Ann's heart began to beat so wildly she thought it would be impossible for her chest to contain it. For the first time she actually believed in Hank's love. She'd actually seen the devastation in his eyes when she'd told him about Melissa. It had been every bit as shattering as her own. He wasn't like the man who'd walked out of her life just because she was having a baby. Hank wasn't afraid of problems. He wanted to face them with her. An unbelievable sense of joy and relief welled up inside her. He was offering her everything she'd ever wanted, everything she'd dreamed of and never dared to expect: love, companionship, strength and family.

Marrying Hank would be a way out. Together they might be able to fight the state's decision about Melissa and adopt her themselves. She wouldn't have to give up her baby. The thought of losing Melissa had affected her more deeply than anything that had happened in the past. Though letting go of other foster children had never been easy, she'd always been able to get beyond the sharp tug of emotion to accept the decisions as being best for the child. But she'd never had Hank in her life before. She'd never felt that she, too, could offer a complete family. She had begun thinking of their relationship as permanent long before this moment and the prospect of losing Melissa had shaken the fantasy. Marrying Hank would allow her to keep it alive.

But was that the only reason she was considering his proposal? If Hank had proposed tonight under any other circumstances, would she have said yes? She couldn't be sure. Only a few days earlier she'd turned him down without hesitation. She almost laughed at the trap in which she'd caught herself. She finally knew without any lingering doubts that Hank was in love with her, was content with what they had found together. She even knew with blinding clarity that she was truly, deeply in love with him. But her motives in marrying him? They would be less than pure.

"I can't, Hank," she whispered finally. "I can't marry you. Not now."

She saw the astonishment register in his eyes, then the flash of hurt. "Why the hell not?"

If she hadn't been so miserable, she might have laughed at his purely masculine indignation. "Because it wouldn't be fair."

"Fair to whom? I love you. There's no doubt about that, right?"

She nodded, believing at last that it was true.

"And you love me? Or am I being too arrogant in assuming that?"

"No. I do," she admitted openly for the first time.

"And it could solve the problem with Melissa?"

"It might."

"Then could you explain for the benefit of my apparently simple brain why we can't get married."

"What if the only reason we're doing it is because of Melissa?"

"Didn't you hear a word I just said? We're in love, Annie. We've admitted it. No more hiding from it. People who are in love get married. They have families. They live happily ever after. It's the thing to do."

She sighed. "I know. It's the timing."

"That is the craziest, most ridiculous, dumbest bit of reasoning I have ever heard in my life," he said, dropping her hands and pacing around the kitchen, bumping into things and knocking them aside until it looked as though a war had been waged in the middle of the room.

"Hank, sit down," she said, deciding she'd better calm him down before he started breaking things.

"I don't want to sit. I want to break things," he said, voicing her fears. As if to demonstrate, he picked up a glass and hurled it across the room. It shattered against the wall. Apparently satisfied with the minimal expression of violence, he calmly walked over and cleaned it up, while Ann just stared at him.

"Feel better?" she said finally.

He dropped the shards of glass into the trash and regarded her sheepishly. "Frankly, no."

"Good. Then you won't bother to break anything else, will you?"

"Don't count on it."

An untimely chuckle emerged from somewhere deep inside her. He scowled ferociously. "I'm sorry," she said at once.

"Annie, what are we going to do about this?"

"We'll think about it. I'm sure with two well-educated brains between us we can come up with a rational decision."

"Maybe that's the problem," he said, suddenly looming over her, his expression fierce. "Maybe we've been too rational about this for too long. Maybe it's time we just acted."

Something about the hungry, determined look in his eyes made her pulse leap and then race wildly. "What do you mean?"

"This," he said, pulling her up and slanting his mouth over hers. His lips were hard and demanding, his tongue persuasive. He backed her against the kitchen counter and pinned her there, his body pressed tight against hers. Ann moaned a halfhearted protest, but it was swallowed by yet another marauding kiss as his hands set her body on fire and melted the last of her resistance. His arousal hard against her set off a sweet ache that grew in intensity until it reached an almost unbearable tension.

Hank slid a hand beneath her skirt, running his fingers along her thigh until he reached the moist heat at the apex. Ann felt the room spin crazily as sensations raced through her. Raw, urgent need sprang to life, tearing away the last shred of sanity. She began frantically working at the buttons on his shirt. Why had he worn the damnable thing tonight of all nights, when she needed to be able to slide his shirt away in one easy movement? When she needed so very badly to touch the rippling muscles beneath? Finally she freed the shirt from his pants. She ran her hands over his chest, then pressed kisses on the heated flesh, finally finding the masculine nipple that was flat and already hard with arousal. She felt Hank tremble as she circled that nipple with her tongue again and again.

The pain that she'd felt when she'd heard that Melissa might be taken away began to ease, lost for the moment in other sensations, the way his flesh came alive beneath her fingers, the warm, musky scent of him.

"Not here, sweetheart," she heard Hank murmur as he slid an arm beneath her knees and lifted her off the floor. When they reached her room, he set her slowly back on her feet, then reached behind her to lock the door and flip on the light.

The trip through the house had restored some of Ann's sanity. "Hank, this is crazy. There are six children in this house."

"Not at the moment."

"Where are they?"

"Out."

"Out where?" she said, then lost track of the question's importance as his lips found an especially sensitive spot behind her knee.

"Oh, my," she gasped softly, her eyes widening.

"That's good?"

"Very good."

"How about here?"

"Hmm."

"And here?"

She giggled and he laughed. "Not so good there," he said. "Okay, how about here?"

Here was . . . incredible, she thought with another gasp of pleasure. The laughter died and the loving became very serious indeed. Here, in his arms, she had no more doubts. Here she forgot about the past, stopped worrying about the future and lived only for the present.

She found herself letting go, allowing her body to soar, relinquishing her hard-won control without fear. Hank would never harm her. He would never take her anyplace he wouldn't go himself. And, as she felt him explode deep inside her, she believed with all her heart that he would never leave her, that their love could see them through anything. That faith sent her over the edge and, clinging tightly to him, she cried out his name in joyous surrender.

Hank propped himself up on his elbow and studied the woman lying next to him. Her cheeks were still flushed, her dark hair damp and feathered around her face. The tips of her breasts were rose-hued and puckered in the chilly air. She was so beautiful, with a radiance that began inside and left her glowing. Her skin was as smooth as ivory. Her lips had the power to tempt him beyond reason. Her slightest touch could heat his body in a way that drove him to distraction. His heart was filled to bursting with the sheer wonder of loving her.

He watched the steady rise and fall of her chest, heard the slight catch in her breath, the gentle sigh.

Her eyes still closed, a smile playing about her still-swollen lips, she said quietly, "This won't solve our problem, you know."

"If you think that, then you haven't been listening."

"Listening?" Her smile grew. "Is this your way of conversing?"

"Can you think of any more intimate form of communication?"

"No, but some people think words cover more ground and offer more clarity."

He shook his head. "Then they've never experienced the language of love." He gently cupped her breast as he gazed into her eyes, his thumb insistently grazing the sensitive peak. "What am I saying now?"

When the color rose in her cheeks and she tried to look away, he tilted her chin up until she was forced to face him.

"I'm saying I love you." He smoothed his hand over the curve of her hip. "And now?"

Ann swallowed convulsively as he continued the slow strokes.

"Well?" he prodded.

"I love you," she said hesitantly.

"Very good. You're catching on."

"Thank you, professor."

"Should I continue?"

"Please do."

He did—and no lesson had ever been more exhilarating, no discussion more thrilling.

And when they were lying tangled together, breathless from experiencing all the nuances of the language of love, he whispered, "Have I made myself clear yet?"

"Very clear."

"Then you'll marry me?"

"Yes," she said finally and without hesitation. "Yes, Hank, I'll marry you."

He grinned at her. "It's about time. I was running out of arguments."

"Somehow I doubt that." She cuddled more closely into his side.

"Annie."

"Hmm?"

"I hate to ruin a good moment, but the kids..."

"Oh, my God!" she said, sitting straight up and pulling the sheet up to her chin.

"Settle down," he soothed. "They're not in the room, but they are likely to be getting home soon and we probably should not be in here."

"Good thinking," she said, gathering up her clothes, which had been flung from one end of the bedroom to the other. "You get out. I'm taking a shower."

He grabbed her hand and pulled her back. "One last kiss."

Her lips were still warm and tasted of salt and musk. It was all he could do to relinquish her. Finally, swatting her gently on the bottom, he said, "Go. I'll meet you in the kitchen."

Fifteen minutes later, they were seated at the kitchen table with the overly done meal in front of them when the truck doors began slamming outside.

"You'd better eat fast," Hank advised. "We were supposed to eat the chicken before it turned to leather."

Ann's eyes widened. "You mean you weren't responsible for all this?"

"Nope. Your sweet, innocent children set the scene tonight for the great seduction. I think they got tired of leaving it to us."

"Are we supposed to tell them how it turned out?"

Hank glanced pointedly at Ann's glowing face and her hastily donned bathrobe. "I don't think we'll have to say a word," he said as the back door creaked open.

Tracy stuck her head in hesitantly. "Don't mind us. I just wanted you to know we're home. We'll go in the front door."

"That's not really necessary," Ann said.

"It's not?" Tracy said, her voice instantly filled with disappointment. "How come?"

"Because this is your house and you don't have to go tiptoeing around in the dark outside."

Tracy glanced at Hank hopefully. "Did you like dinner?"

"It was very special. Now why don't you just go ahead and ask what you really want to know?"

At his teasing tone, a broad grin broke over her face. "Did it work?"

He glanced over at Ann and winked. "That depends on exactly what you had in mind. I did ask Ann to marry me."

There was a barely smothered whoop from the crowd of kids huddling in the dark behind Tracy. The door opened wider and all six faces peered at Ann.

"And?" Jason demanded impatiently.

"I said yes."

"Oh, wow!" Tracy sighed dreamily.

"Fantastic!"

"We're going to be a real family?" David asked.

"A real family," Hank promised. His eyes intent on Ann's, he added, "All of us."

With Hank's promise echoing in her ears, she held out her arms to Melissa, who came running. With a lump in his throat, Hank watched the chubby-cheeked toddler crawl into Ann's lap and lay her head sleepily against Ann's breast. No matter what it took, he vowed to fight for Melissa and win. He would keep them all together.

"I think we should celebrate," Jason said, sounding very mature until his voice skidded up, then back down, in midsentence.

"Good idea," Hank and Ann concurred as Jason opened the refrigerator door, then turned to stare at them, a puzzled expression on his face. "The strawberries and stuff are still in here. What have you guys been doing all this time? We've been gone for hours."

"Jason!" Tracy said. "How dumb are you?"

He immediately blushed a fiery shade of red, then grinned with impish enthusiasm. "I guess it worked pretty good."

"I guess it did," Hank said, reaching over to take Ann's hand. "Better than I'd ever dreamed possible."

Epilogue

The backyard was filled with pink balloons. They were tied to the backs of lawn chairs. Like bunches of colorful coconuts, they dangled from the palm trees. They floated above the redwood picnic table that was laden with brightly wrapped packages.

"Hey, Dad, what do you think?" David called as Hank rounded the corner of the house.

Hank followed the sound of David's voice and finally spotted him high up in the banyan tree. "I think you'd better get down from that tree before your mother catches you and has a heart attack."

"His mother is up here with him," Ann said, parting the branches and peering down at him. Hank's breath caught in his throat. "We're decorating."

"Ann," he began in a choked voice as his heart thumped unsteadily. The woman obviously had nerves of steel. His own had taken a decided beating over the past year.

"Don't be such a worrywart," she chided, lowering herself awkwardly from a sturdy limb to the top rung of a stepladder. "I was climbing ladders long before you came along. Who do you think painted the house?"

That was not a point he cared to discuss while his wife was dangling from a tree. He still hadn't gotten accustomed to the hodgepodge of colors. For the moment, he intended to stick to her tree-climbing activities.

"You were not six months' pregnant at the time," he reminded her, holding the ladder steady as she descended.

"I *am* a little more ungainly than usual," she admitted, patting her swollen belly. "You never answered us. How do the balloons look?"

"Plentiful. Who's blowing them up?"

"Liz. Last time I checked her lips were turning blue. You might want to relieve her."

"I don't do balloons," he said emphatically.

"What exactly do you do?" she teased. "I haven't seen you since breakfast. Have you been hiding?"

"I've been having a long talk with Tracy's new boyfriend."

Ann groaned. "Hank, you have not cross-examined that boy, have you? Tracy will kill you."

"No, she won't," he said smugly. "She gave me the list of questions."

"In that case, did he pass?"

"For a nineteen-year-old with pimples and hair longer than Tracy's, he displays remarkable maturity. If they date no more than once a month, I might consider giving them permission to marry in another five or ten years."

Ann rolled her eyes. "I'm sure she'll appreciate that. Has Jason gotten home yet?"

"He and Paul are inside putting together Melissa's new dollhouse. He's already made several modifications to the original design. Todd's so impressed, he's in there now trying to convince him to study architecture."

"Where's Melissa?"

"With Tommy. They're playing house."

Ann's eyebrows shot up. "Isn't she a little young for that?"

"Apparently not. She thinks Liz and Todd brought Amy especially to play the baby. Amy can't crawl quite fast enough to get away from them." He grinned at her. "Does that account for all of them, mother hen?"

She grinned ruefully. "I suppose so."

He reached out and took her hand. "Then come with me. I have a surprise for you."

"For me? It's Melissa's birthday."

"Just come," he said, leading her in through the front door so they wouldn't be disturbed. When he had her alone, he handed her a thick, official-looking envelope. He'd already examined the contents.

Hope and fear warred in her eyes as she took it. She fingered it nervously, but made no move to take the papers from inside. "Hank?"

"It's official. Melissa's ours."

A smile trembled on her lips and tears streamed down her cheeks. "She's really ours?"

"Really. It says so in black-and-white."

She clutched the envelope tightly, then threw her arms around him. That familiar sense of wonder filled Hank's heart. They had it all, more than he'd ever imagined himself having.

"Hank, isn't this the most wonderful day?" Ann said with a heartfelt sigh. As she rested her head against his shoulder she placed his hand over the swell of her stomach. As if aware of his presence, their baby gave a sure, emphatic kick.

"Definitely a football player," he said with pride.

"A ballet dancer," she countered.

"Why are you fighting?" a little voice asked from the doorway.

"We're not fighting," Ann told Melissa. "We're discussing."

"Mommy tends to discuss rather forcefully," Hank explained as Ann poked him in the ribs.

"Isn't it time for my party yet?"

"It's time, short stuff," Hank concurred. "How about a ride to the backyard?"

Melissa's eyes lit up as Hank swooped her onto his shoulders, then held out his hand to help Ann to her feet.

"Let's go celebrate," he said, his gaze catching Ann's and holding. "Melissa, don't forget to make a wish before you blow out the candles on your cake."

"I already made one last year," she confided, leaning down to peer into his eyes from an upside-down angle.

"And what did you wish for?"

"I wished for a mommy and daddy, and you know what?" She tapped a tiny finger against his lips.

"What?" Hank said, exchanging a look with Ann.

"It worked," she said happily. "I got a mommy and daddy now."

Ann slid her arm around his waist as Hank said, "You sure do, half-pint. And nobody in the whole wide world could love you any more."

Melissa tugged impatiently on his beard. "Now can I open my presents, please?"

He lowered her to the ground. "Go to it, kid."

As Melissa raced across the yard, the whole family gathered around. Ann looked up into Hank's face, her eyes shining. "No matter what's in all those packages," she said, "I don't think there's anything to compare with the gift we got."

"That's right," he agreed, lowering his lips to capture hers. "Ours is going to last a lifetime."

* * * * *

COMING NEXT MONTH

#601 LOVE FINDS YANCEY CORDELL—Curtiss Ann Matlock
Yancey Cordell had every reason to be cynical about Annalise Pardee. Yet the fragile new ranch owner inspired a strange kind of loyalty... and evoked something suspiciously like love.

#602 THE SPIRIT IS WILLING—Patricia Coughlin
Thrust into an out-of-body experience, Jason Allaire landed the unlikely role of guardian angel to adorable oddball Maxi Love. But would earthy masculine urges topple his halo and destroy his second chance at love?

#603 SHOWDOWN AT SIN CREEK—Jessica St. James
LaRue Tate wasn't about to let the government commandeer her precious prairieland. But when "government" fleshed out as handsome, rakish J. B. Rafferty, she faced an unexpected showdown—with her own bridling passions!

#604 GALAHAD'S BRIDE—Ada Steward
Horseman Houston Carder had a heart the size of Texas, with more than enough room for sheltering delicate Laura Warner. But this particular damsel seemed to resist rescue, no matter how seductive the Sir Galahad!

#605 GOLDEN ADVENTURE—Tracy Sinclair
The thrill of being romanced by a mysterious expatriate made it worth missing her boat. Or so thought stranded traveler Alexis Lindley... until she discovered the dashing adventurer was a wanted man.

#606 THE COURTSHIP OF CAROL SOMMARS—
Debbie Macomber
Cautious Carol Sommars successfully sidestepped amorous advances—until her teenage son rallied his best buddy, who rallied *his* sexy single dad, whose fancy footwork threatened to halt the single mom's retreat from romance....

AVAILABLE THIS MONTH:

#595 TEA AND DESTINY
Sherryl Woods

#596 DEAR DIARY
Natalie Bishop

#597 IT HAPPENED ONE NIGHT
Marie Ferrarella

#598 TREASURE DEEP
Bevlyn Marshall

#599 STRICTLY FOR HIRE
Maggi Charles

#600 SOMETHING SPECIAL
Victoria Pade

Silhouette Intimate Moments®

Beginning next month,
Intimate Moments will bring you
two gripping stories by Emilie Richards

Coming in June
Runaway
by EMILIE RICHARDS
Intimate Moments #337

Coming in July
The Way Back Home
by EMILIE RICHARDS
Intimate Moments #341

Krista and Rosie Jensen were two sisters who had it all—
until a painful secret tore them apart.

They were two special women who met two very special men
who made life a little easier—and love a whole lot better—
until the day when Krista and Rosie could be sisters once
again.

You'll laugh, you'll cry and you'll never, ever forget. Don't
miss the first book, RUNAWAY, available next month at your
favorite retail outlet.

Silhouette Books®

RUN-1

Indulge a Little
Give a Lot

A LITTLE SELF-INDULGENCE CAN DO
A WORLD OF GOOD!

Last fall readers indulged themselves with fine romance and free gifts during the Harlequin®/Silhouette® "Indulge A Little—Give A Lot" promotion. For every specially marked book purchased, 5¢ was donated by Harlequin/Silhouette to Big Brothers/Big Sisters Programs and Services in the United States and Canada. We are pleased to announce that your participation in this unique promotion resulted in a total contribution of *$100,000.*

*

Watch for details on Harlequin® and Silhouette®'s next exciting promotion in September.

INS

A BIG SISTER
can take her places

She likes that. Her Mom does too.

BIG BROTHERS/BIG SISTERS AND HARLEQUIN

Harlequin is proud to announce its official sponsorship of
Big Brothers/Big Sisters of America. Look for this poster in
your local Big Brothers/Big Sisters agency or call them to
get one in your favorite bookstore. Love is all about sharing.

BB/BS 1A